THE PAPER MUSEUM

THE
PAPER
MUSEUM

KATE S. SIMPSON

union
square
kids
NEW YORK

**union
square
kids**

NEW YORK

UNION SQUARE KIDS and the distinctive Union Square Kids logo are trademarks of Union Square & Co., LLC.

Union Square & Co., LLC, is a subsidiary of Sterling Publishing Co., Inc.

ISBN 978-1-4549-4383-9 (hardcover)
ISBN 978-1-4549-4384-6 (e-book)

Library of Congress Cataloging-in-Publication Data

Names: Simpson, Kate S., author.
Title: The paper museum / Kate S. Simpson.
Description: New York : Union Square Kids, [2022] | Audience: Ages 8 to 12. | Audience: Grades 4-6. | Summary: In a world where paper is obsolete, twelve-year-old Lydia must solve the disappearance of her parents, save her home and the Paper Museum, and repair her relationship with her best friend before her town descends into chaos and everything is lost.
Identifiers: LCCN 2022014929 | ISBN 9781454943839 (hardcover) | ISBN 9781454943846 (epub)
Subjects: CYAC: Missing persons--Fiction. | Museums--Fiction. | Friendship--Fiction. | BISAC: JUVENILE FICTION / Fantasy & Magic | JUVENILE FICTION / Science Fiction / General | LCGFT: Novels.
Classification: LCC PZ7.1.S565328 Pap 2022 | DDC [Fic]--dc23
LC record available at https://lccn.loc.gov/2022014929

For information about custom editions, special sales, and premium purchases, please contact specialsales@unionsquareandco.com.

Printed in Canada

Lot #:
2 4 6 8 10 9 7 5 3 1

08/22

unionsquareandco.com

Cover design by Melissa Farris
Interior design by Julie Robine

For Bill and Edie and Stewart

Chapter 1

I'D BEEN SCANNING BOOKS with the aer reader every day for the past three months—three months since my parents had vanished without a word. There were fifty-four thousand books in the museum's library, and I was searching for one particular volume. It had to have the answers I needed to find my mother and father.

Even though my uncle was in charge of the museum, and even though I lived here now, no one was allowed to work in the library without an authorized assignment. So my actual project was to find bookmarks left by readers, and to keep an inventory of what material the bookmarks were made of, what they looked like, and what books they were in. That was the official reason I was in the library. But that wasn't the reason I got out of bed each morning, tugged on my blue sweater—worn at the elbows—and padded down the long stone corridor to the museum's vast library. As the book handler machine retrieved and sent back book after book, as the aer reader soaked up word after word and pinged bookmark after bookmark, my parents' quiet, invisible voices urged me on from inside the books.

The last time I saw my parents, my mother was tilting a book toward one of the tall, curved windows. One of the pages had a black-and-white drawing on it, and on the page opposite, at the bottom where a ray of sun lit upon it, a peculiar symbol stood out from the paper: an open book enclosed in a circle. That was the book I needed to find. With it, I might finally have a clue as to where my parents were. I would keep checking, even if it took me until the very last volume to find it.

"Lydia?" Uncle Lem called from the hallway, his familiar scent of honey and lemon drifting into the library. "Supper."

I finished the book I was scanning—no bookmarks, no embossed circle—and made my way to the dining room. Uncle Lem was setting the table, so I went into the kitchen and opened the food programmer. A pesto-scented cloud puffed out, enveloping me in a warm embrace.

As we sat at the table, I slid the aer reader off my thumb and held it out to Uncle Lem. It belonged to the museum, and Uncle Lem liked it back for safekeeping at the end of the day. I should have gotten my own two months ago when I turned twelve, but Uncle Lem hadn't said anything about it, so I didn't ask. I didn't need it anyway. I used the museum's for scanning books and researching, and I wasn't interested in clothes or music or group games or the thousands of other things people used theirs for. And since Jane and I had stopped talking, I didn't have anyone to exchange messages with. If I needed to order toothpaste or socks, Uncle Lem did it for me.

I pulled my hand back before he reached for the aer reader. "Actually, do you mind if I keep it until bedtime? I'd like to get a couple more books done tonight."

Uncle Lem nodded and slid his own thin silver band onto his thumb, flicking his knuckle slightly. He liked to check his aer reader as he ate. As the projection activated on his palm, he ate a forkful of green pasta with his other hand. He always made his projection so large it extended beyond his palm, and I had grown used to reading backwards, so over bites of hot pasta I read the info floating above his hand. He was looking at the same time-tables and star charts he checked every night since I'd come to live with him. A blur of calculations spun in the corner of one of the charts. One equation slowed almost to a stop, which I'd never seen happen before—Uncle Lem shook his hand and the numbers sped back up.

While I drained my apple cider, he frowned at the calculations, muttering to himself. He switched to messages and a crease crossed his forehead. I managed to catch a glimpse of MAYOR'S NEW INITIATIVE—before he turned his aer reader off.

"How are you doing with those bookmarks?" he asked.

"I'm up to forty-eight," I said. I waited for him to ask me about the embossed circle, but he didn't. Whenever I tried to talk to him about finding my parents, he said, "We must do our best to acclimate. Patience must be our guide." I trusted Uncle Lem, but patience was a slow-burning ember in the sole of my shoe.

"If you have time in the next couple of days, compile them into a report, and we can aer-message it to city hall. The mayor is getting worked up about receiving statistics from us." He paused, then cleared his throat. "Pick your favorite bookmark and scan that as the cover."

I knew which one I would use: a soft, bumpy rectangle woven out of pink and lilac thread, with a yellow sun rising in the middle. I found it in a book about a girl kidnapped by a funny giant.

We brought our dishes to the kitchen. Uncle Lem usually put the dishes through the food zapper and I put them back in the cabinet, but today he excused himself, asking if I minded doing them alone. As he hurried out of the kitchen, he turned his aer reader back on, the charts and graphs spinning at a dizzying rate, a blur of reds and oranges.

I did the dishes quickly and headed back to the library.

Uncle Lem found me as I was scanning one last book for the night. I had been thinking of the looks on my parents' faces when I surprised them in the library that last day, my father's twinkly eyes darting back and forth, my mother's usual expression of gentleness sparked with something that reminded me—although I tried to convince myself this wasn't true—of trepidation. "Do you have everything you need?" Uncle Lem asked, looking up from his aer reader, but no, I didn't: I needed my parents back. But he meant for the bookmark project, so I nodded.

"I've put in the order for food deliveries," he said. "And toiletries."

"That's early," I said. "It's not due for four days."

He stepped back into the hallway. "I have some other things I need to arrange." His aer reader blipped and he read the projection. "My brother Renald is coming tomorrow. He'll be staying for a little while."

"He will?" But Uncle Lem had already walked away, clearly intent on his errands. Uncle Renald rarely visited the museum, except for brief visits every couple of years, when he scarfed down food and made an excuse to leave. He lived in one of the cities to the south and had nothing but disdainful things to say about our small town, and our even smaller museum on its outskirts. I barely knew him. I had a hazy memory that he'd once brought a kitten, nestled in a basket, and we'd entertained it with a piece of dolphin-gray string. The memory was so fuzzy and so unlike his otherwise unfriendly behavior, I wondered if it had really happened.

It was odd that he was coming and more odd that he was staying. Other than the fall interns who came for the one-month program, it was unusual for anyone to stay overnight. Before, my parents and I never slept over unless Uncle Lem had to leave on a trip and needed someone to take care of the building. He would only let family watch it for him.

I pressed the button on the book handler machine to send the book back to its shelf, and a flash of cold washed over me like a bucket of freezing water as I realized what this meant. If Uncle Renald was coming, Uncle Lem needed someone to watch the museum. He was going away.

Uncle Lem, my one constant since my parents had disappeared, was leaving me.

CHAPTER 2

THE MUSEUM WAS LOCATED outside of town, beyond the stone wall that had enclosed the area since olden times. A narrow, gravel path lined with trees—some mounted with lamps—meandered to the museum's front gate. While there were transport cubes in town, including one that extended to the nearest city, they did not reach the museum. Once visitors arrived in town, if they wanted to come to the museum, they approached on foot.

Uncle Renald arrived early the next day, his traveling cloak swinging from side to side like a pendulum. He was trailed by a delivery boy from town, who carted a huge piece of luggage to the gate, then turned around so fast dust swirled in his wake. Uncle Renald coughed into the corner of his cloak.

Uncle Lem shook his hand and thanked him for coming on such short notice. I squeaked out a hello that must have been too quiet for him to hear; his head shifted in my direction slightly, but he didn't acknowledge me. Probably better to stay unnoticed, anyway. He carried a small cage. Inside it, a spiky animal sat curled into a ball.

"Oh, what is it?" I said, before I could stop myself.

Uncle Renald rotated and looked directly at me, his bright eyes so similar to my mother's but without any of the warmth hers held. "It's a hedgehog," he said. "And it's not to be tampered with. It's hibernating."

The animal's ears poked up and twitched. It didn't seem like it was hibernating.

"If you could be so kind," Uncle Renald said, pointing a long finger at his luggage. I looked at Uncle Lem, but he was already walking the path to the courtyard that spread in front of the museum. Sighing, I lugged the suitcase, bumping my heel with every step. After depositing the suitcase in one of the spare rooms, I went looking for Uncle Lem, hoping to find him alone.

When I reached the dining room, voices from the kitchen stopped me short. I shouldn't have listened. But instead of turning around, I crawled under the serving window that separated the two rooms, its slated blinds closed but thin enough to hear through.

"This is a dangerous time to leave," Uncle Renald said, but he didn't sound at all frightened. The counter creaked as if he were leaning against it from the other side.

"But you know that's exactly why I need to leave now," Uncle Lem replied. His voice was muffled, like he was bending down to look in the lower cabinets. "The calculations have shifted—I've checked and rechecked them. It's the one opportunity." A sliding noise as the pantry door opened and closed. Feet moved along the floorboards, so close to the counter I could smell Uncle Lem's honeyed citrus lozenge through the window. "I've ordered plenty of supplies and sundries, all you'll need while I'm away. Keep the mayor happy, but don't give him more information than he asks for. The last thing we need is him breathing down our necks." He clicked open the spice cabinet and sneezed. "And please, if the time comes before I return—" He hesitated and spoke too quietly for me to hear.

"We don't need a young girl to do it," Uncle Renald said in a gruff voice. "I can handle it myself."

"No!" Uncle Lem was emphatic. "I'm sorry, Renald, but you can't, not after what happened last time. There can be no experimenting on your part. Promise me you'll give it to Lydia."

"Why don't you give it to her yourself?"

"Renald, you know how important the timing of this is. I trust you'll make the right choice."

Uncle Renald had been at the museum less than twenty minutes, but already I wasn't sure he deserved that trust.

I retreated to the courtyard, the heft of eavesdropping—and Uncle Lem's departure—pressing on me, squeezing my lungs. The air outside was crisp, hinting at the early coolness of fall. Soon the leaves would be changing. The door of the museum opened and closed with a firm *clunk*, and Uncle Lem approached. He was wearing his traveling attire.

"You're leaving already?" I said. "Please don't go." My voice came out thin, a vein on the underside of a leaf.

"I wouldn't go if I didn't have to, Lydia," he said. "Trust me. Renald is the only one who can fill in while I'm gone, but I need you to help him take care of the museum. You must follow his instructions."

"Where are you going?" I didn't dare ask if he was looking for my parents. I wasn't sure I could bear it if he said no.

"A place I've never been before." He smiled, but there was much his smile was not telling me.

"When will you come back?" I asked. "The interns arrive tomorrow!"

"I know you will do your best to welcome them," he said, kissing the top of my head and handing me the museum's aer reader. "I'll be back as soon as I can."

I followed him to the front gate, where strips of jagged clouds streaked the otherwise clear sky. At the end of the road, he adjusted his pack higher on his back and waved, before disappearing.

When I got back inside, Uncle Renald was moving his luggage into Uncle Lem's room. I retreated to the library and scanned, scanned, scanned. Even though I scanned all day long, I found no bookmarks, no circle.

At supper, as Uncle Renald sat at the long dining room table with the meal I had heated, I told him I preferred to eat in the kitchen.

"What is your role here?" he asked me.

"My parents—" I started to say.

"I'm not asking why you are here. I'm asking what you do here."

I gulped. "A bookmark project. In the library. I also do chores to help Uncle Lem: sweeping, programming meals, dusting the display cases . . ." I couldn't finish. His stare was a boulder about to fall on me.

"Dismissed," he said, and I ran to the kitchen.

After cleaning up, I knocked on his door to see if he wanted beds made up in the dormitory for the interns. Uncle Lem had told me two interns were coming, but one was supposed to be Jane, and after our fight and long silence, it was possible she'd changed her mind.

Uncle Renald didn't answer, although I had knocked loudly and it was too early for bed. I gathered sheets and blankets from the linen closet, enough for two beds, and stepped out into the courtyard to cross to the dormitory. The sun was dropping behind the trees, swathes of peach and violet stretching across the sky. It was the kind of sunset that would have made Jane and me race to the tallest tower in the town's wall, running up the spiral stairs so fast we'd be dizzy and out of breath when we reached the top. The light reflecting off the fields and hills and sky would surround us like we were in a bottle filled with stripes of colorful sand. Sounds would float up, the clicks and snaps of shopkeepers closing up for the night, the gentle rumble of townspeople returning home through the transport cube, the beeps of food programmers, and the smells of warm dinner rolls and roasted vegetables. We'd wait until the streetlamps spun on one by one throughout the town, and then turn to watch the dots of light appear along the transport line like a row of fireflies passing a message to the city on the eastern horizon. Then we'd run back down to our houses.

A cool draft rustled the leaves of a maple tree and brought me back to the squat façade of the dormitory and the stack of bedclothes in my arms. The breeze caught the corner of the top sheet, raising it up slightly in an uncertain wave, caught between goodbye and hello, between what was and what was to come.

CHAPTER 3

I ROSE EARLY THE next morning and sat outside among the chatter of birds, my sweater wrapped tightly around me. The birds flew from tree to tree as if they didn't know what it was like to miss their parents, their uncle, or their best friend. Their beaks were full with raspberries plucked from the thorny bushes planted at the edge of the courtyard, the air sweet with the scent of overripe fruit.

I used the museum's aer reader to check aer logs for any news of my parents, as I did every morning. There were notes of missing and found people, none of whom matched my parents, especially since Uncle Lem wouldn't let me file a missing persons report for them. My parents had long ago disabled the geolocation capability on their aer readers, so there was no easy way to trace where they might be, but I checked every live feed I could access, in case they walked by in the background. News outlets were full of complaints about a spike in mixed-up deliveries and slowdowns at the transport cubes. Nothing useful. There was never anything. My parents had simply vanished.

A brown wren landed on a low branch and chirped until I looked at her. As soon as I did, she chirped again, then flew off behind the museum in the direction of the dogwood fort hidden in the woods, a place where I had spent many hours playing, and, after my parents disappeared, many hours crying—often with Jane at my side. I hadn't been back since our fight. The fort felt out of reach, a place of solace I didn't deserve to have.

The empty branch swayed from the wren's takeoff.

I turned the aer reader to the projection for the mayor's office. It took only a couple of steps to find the tab for reporting a missing person. Uncle Lem had insisted we didn't need to do this, but he wasn't here now. My parents *were* missing, and I had to do what I could to find them.

My fingers tapped the air lightly, filling in the requested information: name, address, physical description, date last seen. First my mother, then my father, then I took a deep breath and pressed SUBMIT. An automated reply popped up, confirming the submission. Then a second screen popped up, with bold letters:

MISSING PERSONS HAVE THIRTY DAYS TO ACTIVATE THEIR AER READERS, AFTER WHICH ALL ASSOCIATED ACCOUNTS WILL BE DELETED, AND HOUSING WILL BE REASSIGNED. A picture of our house in town floated underneath.

A wave of panic rippled from my stomach to my toes. What had I done?

There was no DELETE button, no UNDO. My fingers scrambling, I sent a message to the mayor's office, asking them to ignore my report, to please cancel it. And what did it mean by "activate their aer readers"? My parents disliked being dependent on aer readers and tried to use them as little as possible, but they were necessary for so many things that surely, wherever they were, they'd use them within the month.

Thirty days. They'd already been gone for three times that long. They *had* to come back soon. I tried not to think that they had been kidnapped, or somehow simultaneously developed amnesia. If I could find the book my mother had been holding, I'd have a clue as to where they were. It had to have something to do with their disappearance or they wouldn't have been acting so strange about it. The book wouldn't be something as obvious as *The Best Place to Disappear for Three Months*, but it would show me what they'd been working on, what they'd been thinking about, what direction they may have gone in. I had to find that book.

I headed to the library to scan.

I wanted to scan at least fifty books before the interns arrived, and scanned so fast that the aer reader felt sluggish. I barely took in the stories, but the images filled my mind: moss-covered mansions in fields, a window made of rainbow shards, a snail shell so big a human could live in it, an underwater forest of golden trees. But still no circle. And no more bookmarks.

When I had five books left until my quota, Uncle Renald cleared his throat in the doorway.

"Check that everything's ready, then sweep the courtyard," he said. I sent back the book I'd been scanning. I'd have to find extra minutes later to catch up.

I double-checked to make sure the beds in the dormitory were free of wrinkles. In the kitchen, even though I had already peeked at it a dozen times, I made sure the food programmer light was on. The meal was programmed for extra people, as I had no idea if the interns' parents would be staying to eat.

The families arrived on the hour, their knocks on the gate and their *hallos?* stretching into the courtyard. But Uncle Renald reclined on a bench with his aer reader, his thumb moving deftly over his palm, ignoring them. When I moved toward the gate, he shook his head *no*. This was not the kind of welcome Uncle Lem would have given them.

After I had swept every corner of the courtyard and begun to dust the stone wall that surrounded it, Uncle Renald—without getting up from his seat—finally nodded.

A weed, tall and skinny like Uncle Renald, had sprouted on the path to the front gate. I yanked it out and tossed it behind the trees that lined the path.

My hands shook as I unlocked the door in the gate, focusing on the key and the coldness of the iron. "I'm sorry for the delay," I said quietly into the air, and when I dared to look up to see if Jane was among the interns, and, if she was, whether she was scowling or smiling at me, her mother breezed through the gate and pulled me close.

"Lydia!" she said. "How we've missed you!" Her warmth almost overwhelmed me. But I remembered my duties and pulled away, then curtsied—the official museum welcome to interns.

When I rose, Jane gave me a small, tight smile, not the one that filled her face, but I would take anything. I tried not to grin back at her. That was easier to do when I thought of the last time I had seen her, how I had shouted at her like a volcano spurting hot rocks.

Hopefully, the fact that she was here for the intern program meant she had forgiven me. Or, since she had signed up before my outburst, maybe it had been too late for her to back out.

I gestured for the other intern and her guardian to come through, curtsying to them as well.

The girl wore an aquamarine dress and what appeared to be eyeglasses with no glass in them, just large oval frames. "We've sure been waiting awhile!" she said as she strolled through the gate, a prim-looking lady in a business suit following her. A boy with freckled arms who smelled strongly of pine soap waited with a third woman. The boy held a suitcase that he switched from one hand to another.

Why were there three interns instead of two? After the disregard he had shown toward the visitors' presence so far, I did not think Uncle Renald would be delighted at this news.

I led them to the courtyard as slowly as I could.

CHAPTER

4

UNCLE RENALD STOOD IN front of the museum. The interns and their families stopped in the middle of the courtyard as though a line had been painted there. They probably expected a word of introduction or a tour of the museum. But Uncle Renald stood firm, his feet touching at the heels, as welcoming as a slab of granite.

When he noticed that there were three young people with luggage, his back stiffened more than usual. "Your proof of acceptance," he said. Jane stepped forward first, then the other girl, then the boy, each flashing their aer readers.

The adults shuffled back and forth in their small group, but even after sniffing at each of the interns' aer readers, Uncle Renald stood there without opening the museum door.

The girl with the glasses held up her aer reader to take a picture, tapping the shutter button repeatedly then jumping back when it took a rapid-fire series of photos. "Wow, it works great here!" she said. "I didn't expect that in an old place like this." She laughed.

Uncle Renald did not look amused. Instead, he coughed and said, "No aer readers are allowed inside. Kindly return them to your guardians for the duration of your internship."

The girl dropped her shoulders and frowned, but Uncle Renald didn't budge. Jane handed hers to her mother. The boy fumbled in his pocket and his aer reader fell to the ground. As he picked it up, a faint humming sound emanated from it. The girl was the last to turn hers over. The adults pocketed the aer readers silently.

I tried not to stare as Jane hugged her mother goodbye.

The girl intern, instead of saying goodbye, sidled up next to me, staring at the museum's aer reader hooked onto my thumb. "At least you still have one," she whispered loudly.

Uncle Renald turned toward me. "That one too," he said.

"Sorry?" I asked, almost certain I had heard him wrong. But he held out his palm. "But I need this for—" I stopped short as his face darkened, and I dropped it into his hand without another word. Surely he'd give it back to me later so I could keep scanning the books. This was just for show.

Uncle Renald addressed the parents. "Thank you for your visit. Interns will not be allowed to leave museum grounds until the conclusion of the internship, at which point you may pick them up at the front gate." After the parents departed, Uncle Renald said, "Food," and we followed him through the museum's front door and into the dining room. Jane and the other interns put their luggage under the long window that filled the room and pulled out chairs while I hurried into the kitchen to gather the food. It was hot and waiting—there would be plenty of leftovers.

After depositing the food, I hesitated, but Uncle Renald motioned for me to choose a chair at the table, while he stood at the head. Everyone was silent, watching him, and when he sat down, sweeping his long vest to the side to avoid sitting on it, we all sat too. We ate entirely in silence, except for forks clinking against plates, and glasses being set back on the table. I both longed for and dreaded conversation. Uncle Lem had told me to welcome the interns—we should go around the table and say our names, at least.

Finally daring to speak, I opened my mouth, but Uncle Renald cut me off with a short bark of a cough. So I sneaked peeks at the interns between bites, trying to look friendly when I wasn't chewing, and when Uncle Renald finished his meal he stood up, his chair scraping the floor.

"Interns should now go to bed," he said, "and report for duty at seven o'clock in the courtyard." Then he left. There was no tour, even for them, which I assumed they would have liked so as not to spend their first night in completely foreign surroundings. They at least needed to know where they'd be sleeping. It was up to me, then, to show them to the dormitory.

After Uncle Renald's heavy footfalls faded away to his room, I started gathering plates. Jane stood to help me, and the boy picked up his own dishes. The girl with the glasses followed us into the kitchen empty-handed.

We should have known one another's names by now, and I wasn't sure how to cross the bridge of overdue introductions. Instead, everyone watched while I put the dirty dishes under the food zapper—ours was an old-fashioned model. The boy intern leaned in to watch the beam shooting out and dissipating the left-over food and germs.

As he turned back to me, I plunged my hand in his direction. "My name is Lydia," I said, breaking the silence.

"I'm Karl," he said, shaking my hand.

"Florence," said the girl intern, turning from the cupboard she'd been peeking in and smiling a smile too big for her face.

"I'm Jane," said Jane, and we all looked around at one another.

Trying to make my voice warm to cover the strangeness of their visit so far, I added, "Welcome to the Paper Museum."

"It's so quaint here!" Florence said. "You store all your kitchen items on-site?"

"Yes," I said. "We don't have any transport cubes at the museum." The trend in the cities—both the large city to the east that governed our town, where the mayor's office was, and the cities to the south—was to send items to a warehouse for storage when they weren't being used, and to retrieve them each time they were needed. The transport cubes for objects made this a quick process, but it was somewhat expensive, and even though some people liked the clean, empty look of having nothing on hand, I preferred having what I needed within reach. Our house in town was the same way, full of familiar and well-used items, as were most of my neighbors' houses, although before I moved to the museum I had started to hear more and more often the soft *zurr zurr* of objects being transported in the cubes.

When the dishes were put away, Jane, Florence, and Karl carried their luggage—and I carried an extra set of bedding—to the dormitory. Inside, I spun the light on in the short hallway that led to the common room, which had individual bedrooms coming off it like the spokes of a wheel. The common room had several couches and low tables, with shelves underneath holding bins of games, as well as brushes and paint pots. In most homes, one wall would have an aer screen, but here the wall was filled with the painted outline of a cityscape. The mural was splashed with a mishmash of colors and patterns, designs left behind by previous interns. I had always thought it was a scene of a single, unknown city, until I began to recognize some of the shapes and spires, and realized they were an amalgam of structures from all over, buildings that still stood, some that were now destroyed or flooded, and some that were mythical.

"You can add to the mural while you're here, if you'd like," I said.

"Great," Karl said. He poked around while I snapped the sheets onto one of the remaining beds, and Jane and Florence unpacked.

After a while, everyone filtered back into the common room, and I lingered, torn between staying to make sure they were settled and trying to get the museum aer reader back from Uncle Renald so I could finish those five books before bed.

Florence flopped onto the couch. "Your dad isn't exactly the friendliest guy around, is he?" she asked.

"He's *not* my father," I said, more forcefully than I intended.

"Then who is he?" Florence asked.

"My uncle."

"Oh," she said, as if that didn't make any difference in the world. As if it didn't matter who my father was, or my mother, two people who meant so much to me.

"What other internships are you doing, Karl?" Jane asked, and I was grateful that she changed the subject.

He was fiddling with one of the gadgets in the game bucket, but looked up at the sound of his name. "Architecture, road repair, medicine, textiles, zoology, history, agriculture, budgeting, and bread baking. And here. Was that ten?"

The interns had a hundred places to apply to, in many different categories. They spent a month each in ten places before taking the determination exam and finding out where they best fit. Very few interns came to the museum, and the ones who came mostly applied late or hadn't gotten into the places they wanted. No interns ever landed permanently at the museum—our family had been running it alone for generations.

"What about you?" Karl asked Jane. She looked down at her hands before answering.

"Still waiting to hear back," she said. Which was odd, because usually interns found out about all their assignments at once.

"Are you doing any internships?" Karl asked me.

I shook my head quickly. Jane's eyes were on me, but I couldn't face her. I was scared to see that same hurt look from the day we'd fought. She had been such a good friend to me. After my parents first vanished, she had come to visit many times, sharing bits of cheese strudel her mother had baked, pretending not to see that by the time the pastry made it to my mouth, it was soaked with tears. But that was before the day we sat under the dogwood tree and she told me she wouldn't be able to come for a while because she had to help at home while her mother visited Grandma Hastings up north. The day she had tried to pry me from the museum.

"Come to town with me," she had said, playing with a red kousa berry that had fallen from the tree. "There's a festival tonight by the river." She tossed the berry up gently and caught it in her palm.

"I can't," I said.

She pushed her shoulder into mine gently. "Come on, Lydia, you can't stay here all the time. If your parents come back, Curator Lem will get you right away—"

"I can't," I said again, more forcefully. The river festivals were my father's favorite. He'd bring his vielle and bow and we'd sit by the riverbank, my mother and I dipping our heels in and out of the dark water while the music floated on the current.

"There will be flat cakes with drizzle," Jane said.

My father had promised to teach me the notes on his instrument.

Jane added, "We'll keep an eye out for your parents." She stood up and held her hand out. "Come on, let's go."

"I can't!" I shouted, the words exploding out of me. "They wouldn't be at the festival without me! They wouldn't *go* without me! I've looked and looked for them and I can't find them, so I have to wait for them here—I can't leave the museum! I promised them I'd be here! Why can't you understand that?"

She backed away, but I kept shouting. I was a thunderstorm of words, all the fear and anger and frustration I had felt since my parents disappeared banging together and striking her. Even though what I was saying was hurtful and she was only trying to help me, I couldn't stop the barrage of words. "I promised them!" I shouted. "And you're trying to make me leave—I don't need a friend like you! Just go! I never want to see you again!" Jane burst into tears and ran away.

That had been over a month ago. As I looked at her now across the common room, I wondered if she thought of me as the Lydia who sat under the flowering dogwood and cried and shouted and raged, or if she remembered the better times—the fun we had when we lived next door to each other in town, sharing toys and trinkets and secret signals through open windows past bedtime.

"Do you get a lot of visitors here?" Florence's voice rang out.

I shook my thoughts clear and tried to remember the museum's last visitor. There was very little interest in paper and paper artifacts. Information was stored and shared through aer readers, and paper or boxes for packaging had been replaced by plasticress, a sturdy, reusable material that stretched to fit objects of any size and could shrink down as small as a fingerprint when not being used. Paper was bulky and obsolete, which many people seemed to think meant it was boring. But we did have one visitor over the summer. The mayor's office had sent a marketing agent to the museum, claiming they needed a new logo of the museum for promotional listings. A lady had come one afternoon and taken pictures and researched in the library. When I peeked in at her, she seemed entirely uninterested in the job, uploading images from random books to her aer reader without really looking at them. We hadn't had any visitors since then.

I honestly didn't know why more people didn't visit. The books in the library and the items in the display cases were fascinating—I had spent hours looking at them and sometimes felt I was seeing them for the first time. It was amazing to think these thin pieces of what used to be trees had been touched by other people, written on by other hands, and read by other minds, and that the words and stories they contained meant something to people across different times and places. And to have so many in one place: it made the museum itself enchanting. When I was little and visited here with my parents, every time I crossed through the gate and into the courtyard I was covered with welcoming vibrations, a thousand tiny wings brushing my skin. "The air is humming!" I used to say. Since moving here, even though I adored the museum's collection, I didn't feel the humming the same way. Perhaps I had grown too accustomed to it; perhaps it had disappeared when my parents did.

Florence stifled a yawn, and I realized that I hadn't answered her question. "No," I said. "We don't have a lot of visitors. But we do have open visiting hours every Saturday."

She nodded but raised her eyebrows in a slow, uninterested way, and Jane and Karl looked toward their rooms. I took that as my cue to leave. After having spent so much time mostly by myself lately, it was hard to interact with other people. And I couldn't let them distract me from getting through the books. When I knocked on Uncle Renald's door to ask about the aer reader, however, there was no answer. The books would have to wait, no matter how much I wanted otherwise.

CHAPTER 5

THE INTERNS GATHERED IN the courtyard at seven o'clock and waited for Uncle Renald, who sauntered over from the direction of the gate, finishing a stroll around the museum property. I stood off to the side, not wanting to align myself with Uncle Renald but also not part of the group of interns.

Florence peeked over at me with a bright smile. "The gardens here are so lovely. I adore flowers."

I smiled. I loved them too. "There's a book in the library with close-up photos of rare varieties. And it explains the symbolism of different flowers—for instance, daffodils stand for good fortune or hope. Maybe you'd like to see the book while you're here?"

"Sure," she said. "By the way, where's the fountain?"

I twisted around, not sure what she was talking about. "There isn't one."

She wrinkled her forehead but said nothing, because Uncle Renald was glaring at her.

"You will be given a brief tour of the museum," he said, "and then your daily assignment."

I had no idea what projects he planned to assign them. Uncle Lem gave interns a choice and, more often than not, they chose to do research in the library, with its rows and alcoves of shelves stretching up and across, a place that was somehow both cavernous and cozy, especially when the afternoon sun slanted through the windows and warmed the rugs on the stone floor. They could choose from the bountiful array of books, scanning them in the book handler machine as I did, or reading them slowly in the book cradles, which held the books at an angle designed to minimize wear and had a mechanism for turning pages. And, possibly, once they were wearing the proper equipment—flexible plasticress finger pads—the interns could turn the pages themselves.

Other interns chose to work in the Display Room, examining the cases of artifacts the museum had amassed: handwritten letters folded into matching envelopes, instruction manuals for antiquated kitchen equipment, spelling tests, and illustrated poems. There was also the Mechanical Devices Room, which was really two small rooms. Uncle Lem had arranged the first room into a square of display cases that followed the perimeter of the room, starting closest to the door with the earliest of implements—feathers and inkpots—and moving along the wall toward displays of wax crayons, animal-shaped erasers, and staplers. In the middle of the room was a gigantic printing press, its oversized wooden frame holding court over the pens and pencils. I'm not sure Uncle Lem or Uncle Renald knew how the press worked, if it even did.

The second part of this room, accessed through a doorless opening in the back, had been my favorite room since my first visit to the museum: the Typewriter Room. There were fourteen typewriters, all different models—Remington, Royal, Underwood, Olympia, Smith-Corona, Olivetti, and more—arranged by color, a muted rainbow of blacks and grays and light blues spreading across the room. One very lucky person, a long time ago, had been allowed to type a sample sentence onto a square of paper tucked into each typewriter. The same nine words fourteen times: *The quick brown fox jumps over the lazy dog.* It was a lovely sentence, a pangram, containing all twenty-six letters of the alphabet, a way to test each key and demonstrate the shape and style of its type. I had stared at the words for so many hours, examining the different ways the letters curled at the tops and bottoms and stretched between themselves, that it felt like each typewriter had a unique personality, and together they made up a neighborhood of friends.

Uncle Lem had promised me a piece of paper of my own, with words typed on it using one of the typewriters from the museum's collection. He was even going to let me type on the keys myself someday, maybe if one of the inked samples grew too faded to read or if we ever acquired a new typewriter. I longed for someday. I practiced typing in the air, my fingers inches above the typewriter keys and moving as swiftly as stalks of grass blowing in the wind, back and forth: *The quick brown fox jumps over the lazy dog.* My father caught me doing it one day, but instead of scolding me or laughing, he simply nodded.

Those four rooms—the library, the Display Room, the Mechanical Devices Room, and the Typewriter Room—made up the bulk of the museum. The other rooms were the kitchen, the dining room, a parlor that went mostly unused, Uncle Lem's bedroom and office—now occupied by Uncle Renald—and a few utility rooms, storage rooms, closets, and spare rooms, one of which had been transformed into my bedroom.

Before Uncle Renald gave the interns a tour of the museum, he led them to the kitchen and made them scrub their hands up to their elbows, and then he would only let them peek into the rooms, not walk around and examine objects and take their time, as Uncle Lem would have encouraged. Then he assigned their projects for the day.

Karl was to guard the library.

Florence was to guard the Mechanical Devices Room.

And Jane was to guard the Display Room.

By "guard," it turns out, Uncle Renald meant do nothing but stand outside the room for the entire day and make sure no one went in. "Except myself, of course," he said, and, his eyes flicking to me, "and Lydia, if necessary." I wasn't sure who else he thought would go in. We didn't exactly have visitors banging down the front gate.

Standing outside a room for a day was so cruel and boring that I felt compelled to speak up for them. But before I could say anything, Florence raised her hand, and when Uncle Renald gave her an icy nod, she said, "Excuse me, sir, what will we learn by doing this?"

Uncle Renald did not answer right away. Instead, he inspected the pad of his thumb. Finally he spoke, dragging out each word, "If you do your job well, you will learn the value of what is inside the room."

Florence made a face but did not ask any more questions.

As the interns went about their guarding, I did my chores—sweeping the halls, programming the food for the day, then pulling weeds in the courtyard—moving quickly so I could get back to my unfinished books in the library. Uncle Renald was sitting in the sun in the courtyard, using his aer reader in plain sight. I hoped this meant he was open to returning the museum's aer reader to me.

"Uncle Renald," I said, and waited for him to look up. When he didn't, I added, "Sir." He glanced up, his thumb paused in midair. "May I please have the museum aer reader back to continue my project?"

"No," he said, and his thumb moved rapidly again.

"But Uncle Renald, I need it to—"

"To what? Find bookmarks?"

I swallowed. Uncle Lem had assigned me the bookmark project to authorize my search. Uncle Renald didn't know why I really needed to go through the books; he knew only the official reason. It was so much more than finding bookmarks, but I couldn't tell him about the embossed circle and the book my mother was holding. And I definitely couldn't tell him about needing to check that a missing persons report had been withdrawn.

"Yes," I said. "To find bookmarks." Unsaid words swirled inside me.

"A frivolous pursuit," he said. "Your time is better spent monitoring the interns."

"I need it," I said, then paused. If I angered Uncle Renald, he'd never agree to what I wanted, so I had to reason with him instead. "The mayor requested a project update. And Uncle Lem will want to see my progress when he returns."

"I am the curator now," Uncle Renald said. "And if my brother returns and if he thinks your project is worth continuing, then that is a matter for another time. As for the mayor, I continue to be unimpressed by his demands and his new initiative. If he is

determined to find fault with us, so be it. We are beyond his jurisdiction. The most he can do is harass us."

I wasn't sure which of his comments to absorb first. What did
he mean *if* Uncle Lem returned? Of course he'd return. Hopefully,
any day now. But I couldn't wait even one day to continue scanning the books. And what was the mayor's new initiative?

"Uncle Renald—" I tried again.

"*No*," he said, the single syllable a hammer striking a rock. I
turned away without another word.

Without the aer reader, my only option was to look through
the books by hand instead of scanning them, which would be ago-
nizingly slow.

Yesterday I was five books behind. Now I would be ten times
that. Each unscanned book—each day that passed without revealing the hidden book circle—was a brick in the wall that separated
me from my parents.

But I had to keep going. Karl stood outside the library and
nodded politely at me when I went in. "Everything okay?" he
asked. "Do you need help with anything?"

"I need an aer reader," I said. My words must have come out
rude, which I hadn't intended, because Karl made a short choking
sound.

The air in the library, usually pleasantly almond-scented,
smelled like musty tapestries. My station was at the corner of the

big table. Without an aer reader, I had to manually program the book handler machine for the book I wanted, but at least I remembered where I had left off when Uncle Renald interrupted me the day before. I sat, and the book appeared in front of me. Normally I'd leave it in the book handler and flick the aer reader over it— the entire book would be scanned in a matter of minutes, a summary of the contents flashing as a projection, pinging what I had programmed it to be on the lookout for: bookmarks or embossed circles. Instead, I pressed the button that released the book to the nearby cradle, then I pressed the button that opened to the first page and began scanning with my eyes.

Several hours later, I had found no bookmarks or circles, and barely made a dent in the shelf because no matter how fast I told myself to go, I couldn't stop myself from reading all the words on each page. It was a fascinating story about a young prince and a poor boy who looked like twins and switched places. When I was younger and visited the museum with my parents, I spent hours in the library reading books directly, but I had been scanning quickly for so long now I had forgotten what it felt like to delve into a book. Instead of broad themes and characters and plotlines flitting across the aer reader projection, there was so much life in the descriptions I could almost see and hear and smell them myself. It was a shame it took so long, because if I wanted to make any progress, I needed to skim them instead.

I wished I knew which book I was looking for, or that I could concentrate and feel which shelf it was on. It couldn't hurt to try. I sat back in the chair and closed my eyes. I relaxed my shoulders and cleared my mind to make room for a tugging sensation, one particular book willing me to find it. With my eyes closed, the room felt draftier; the birds outside seemed to sing louder. But I felt nothing. Instead, an image floated by: me finding the book, opening it, and realizing it held no clues, no answers. It was just a regular book.

I jerked my eyes open and rubbed them. As my vision came back into focus, a thin blue book from under one of the windows caught my attention. It seemed like a cruel joke, but I sent the book handler for it anyway.

It was not the right book. It was a cookbook called *The Frugal Housekeeper* and did not have a circle. But as the book flipped to the inside back cover, a creased sheet of paper stuck out, held on at one end by some sort of sticky residue. I unfolded the loose end carefully. Along the side, in curled writing, was a list of names: Plitvice, Kaieteur, Ban Gioc-Detian, Victoria, Gullfoss, Niagara, Yosemite, Iguazu, Angel.

Most of the names were unfamiliar, but a few I had heard in school. They were waterfalls.

My parents loved waterfalls, and we often picnicked near small ones close by—but they would never have written in a book.

37

And the pasted paper and the book seemed incredibly old. I wasn't sure what to make of it. This paper didn't seem to be a bookmark, since it was attached to the back cover, so I didn't need to note it for my project, not that I could without the aer reader.

It was noontime, so I pressed the button on the book cradle that transferred the book back to the book handler, which returned the book to its assigned spot on the shelf, then I brought the interns their lunches. They ate standing up outside the rooms they were guarding. After I had cleared and cleaned their plates, Uncle Renald told them to switch rooms. I went to check on them in their new posts, and Jane smiled at me, but she was standing slightly crooked, shifting her weight away from her left side.

"Is your ankle bothering you?" I asked. She had injured her foot years ago at a stilt tournament, and sometimes it acted up. "I'll get you a seat."

"No, no, I'm fine," she said, but I had already moved to a nearby storage closet to grab a stool. As I positioned it against the wall outside the library door, she protested that she didn't need it, but sank onto it all the same. "Is there no word from your parents?" she asked softly, bending down to rub her ankle.

"No," I said, biting my lip to keep my eyes from watering. "And now Uncle Lem has gone somewhere too." I wanted to tell her about the missing persons report, but I couldn't bring myself to mention it when our argument at the dogwood tree stood between us. Instead, I said, "Have you heard anything about the mayor's initiative?"

She lifted her foot and rested it across her knee. "Is that the thing on the news about the giant dome he wants to build? With an indoor river and a woodland park?"

That did sound somewhat familiar. I had come across articles on the aer reader about a new park, but I skimmed over them because they didn't pertain to my parents. Maybe I should have read them more closely.

"It's supposed to be huge," Jane said. "People are excited about it. I guess he's narrowing down the best place to put it."

The museum was surrounded by hundreds of acres of woods. A perfect spot, if the mayor could prove we weren't useful enough to keep around.

"Thanks," I said, realizing this was the most I'd talked to Jane since we'd fought.

"Thank you for the stool," she said.

When I checked on Florence, she wasn't outside the Display Room where she should have been. I looked in the bathroom but it was empty, so I went back to the doorway. A *clink* sounded from inside the room, and when I went in, she was crouched in front of one of the display cases, flicking her fingernail against the glass case.

"What are you doing?" I said, unable to keep my voice from shaking. "You can't do that!" She stood up and smiled at me, then sauntered over to another display case.

"I got bored, that's all," she said.

"Uncle Renald would be furious," I said.

She laughed. "What would he do, make me stand outside a room all day?"

I didn't answer. "I'm teasing," she said. "Where did all this old stuff come from anyway?" She swirled a finger in the general direction of the display case in front of her, then placed it right above the Coconut Tyme matchbook.

"Leave it alone," I whispered. She walked back to her spot by the door.

While Florence had no way of knowing it, the matchbox meant more to me than she could ever realize.

CHAPTER 6

THE OLD AND USELESS Things Market was held once every decade. I was almost ten when it came to town, the square filled with the tinkle of tin bells strung overhead, people buzzing in and out of stalls, and the smell of warm, sugared hucklefruit.

"If we get separated," my mother had said, squeezing my hand, "if you ever can't find us, promise me you'll wait for us at the museum. It's safe there, and you can stay with Uncle Lem."

"I will, I promise," I said, nodding slowly, transfixed by the buckets of sawtooth keys, the bins of rectangular badge holders hanging from lanyards, the piles of early-model aer readers as big as fists.

"Lydia, look at this!" my father said, holding up a pink fishing pole, something I had read about but never seen.

This place was bustling with noises and smells—and I had a tight grip on my mother's hand. The last thing on my mind was getting lost.

"If you see anything made from paper—" my mother whispered. She didn't have to finish her sentence. I knew what to do.

We walked slowly from stall to stall, taking everything in. Many objects were in disrepair and truly useless, piles of forgotten ideas rusted together. While my mother sorted through stacks of worn, colored cloth and my father played with a game of plastic red and black circles, I looked through a bin of random items. Bubble wands, headbands with cat ears, empty picture frames. As I shifted aside a metal pipe shaped like a bent elbow, a strip of white flashed. I picked it up, tilted it, and gasped. A piece of crumpled paper was shoved inside the curve, with a piece of cardboard wedged next to it. Even though I didn't dare take the pieces out myself, without taking my eyes off them I fished in my pocket for a finger pad and put it on in case my hand slipped and touched the paper. Cupping the pipe as if it were a diamond, I sidled over to my parents and showed it to them.

"Wonderful!" my mother exclaimed quietly, clasping her hands together. "Uncle Lem will be so pleased!"

My father nodded quickly to hide his enthusiasm. If the stall-keeper noticed how much we liked it, he might charge us more.

We continued searching but found nothing else made of paper. My father was particularly interested in a triangular silver vial with a matching lid, so we brought that and the curved pipe up to the payment booth. My mother flicked her thumb to activate her aer reader and waved it over the vial and pipe to pay for them.

Once we were outside the booth, the happiness burst out of me. "I found something!" I said. "To put in the museum!" My skirt spun around me as I twirled in the middle of the market.

My parents laughed.

Nearby, a man in a flannel vest chuckled. "A happy family, how wonderful to see! Come closer, and I will show you sights that will keep you laughing all day." He pointed to a booth behind him—a canvas tent draped over poles, plasticress boxes sitting unpacked. A fringed purple blanket was flung over a chair.

"What kind of sights?" my father asked, peering at the half-finished booth.

"All kinds," the man said. "Coin tricks, conjuring, spells—"

"You're not from around here, are you?" my mother interrupted.

"Just passing through, ma'am, but I've come a long distance and I've many fine tricks to demonstrate, for the right price."

"Best you pack up and be on your way," my father said in a low voice. "For your own sake. Magic isn't allowed here."

"I'd like to see a magic trick," I said. "I've never seen one."

"Let's move along," my father said.

Once we were on the path to the museum, the wonders of the market behind us, my mother handed me the pipe, secured in a plasticress travel box. "Why don't you run ahead and show Uncle Lem what you found today?" she suggested. I skipped, holding the box in front of me as if it were a delicate, green-veined chrysalis clinging to a branch.

Uncle Lem was in the courtyard setting a tray of meringue cookies on the table built into the stone wall. "Lydia!" he said, turning as I came closer. "Have you found something?"

I had no breath for words; instead, I thrust the box at him. He took it and pressed the OPEN button. A smile spread across his face. "Marvelous," he said. "Let's get to work."

There was a carrel set up in one of the library alcoves with Uncle Lem's work tools. We both put on fresh finger pads, then Uncle Lem used an extractor to inch the piece of cardboard out of the pipe.

It was a matchbook, with a drawing of coconuts with clocks for faces. The words "Coconut Tyme" were written above the picture. Lifting the cover revealed two matches attached inside.

The crumpled piece of paper was much more of a challenge. It was jammed in, and the last thing we wanted to do was rip it while getting it out. Uncle Lem ran a laser line as close as he could along the edge of the pipe and disintegrated the excess metal. With a minuscule air blower, he meticulously and gently forced the paper out of its spot. When the wrinkled ball was free, he put it in a special machine for flattening pages, usually ones that were damaged by water. He let me press the button, and the ball of paper unfurled in slow motion like a flower blooming.

It was a coloring page. In black and white, a trio of fairies circled a garden. There was a splash of color on the page: one of the flowers had been filled in with pink, purple, and green. I tried to imagine what it must have felt like to grip a colored pencil or crayon and put color on that page, to make even that small piece of it come alive. I tried not to be jealous of whoever had done it.

"Let's find a spot for these," Uncle Lem said, and I shook the strange feeling out of my mind. It was enough to be able to see the paper, to take care of it.

In the Display Room, Uncle Lem keyed the code into one of the cases and lifted the heavy glass lid. He put the matchbook between an instruction manual for a plastic brick set and a shell-shaped fan made of strips of dictionary pages. The coloring page he put in the corner of the next case, near an illustration of a farm scene taken from a children's book. "Wonderful," he said, lowering the lid of the second case. "We'll get some plasticress labels made up as soon as we can. Don't they look lovely in their new homes?"

They certainly did.

"Help me fetch the lemonade, and we'll celebrate out in the sun," Uncle Lem said. Before following him to the kitchen, I lingered to greet my favorite objects in the room: a miniature kite made of colored tissue paper, a yellowed Scrabble game score sheet, and a note unfolded from a triangle that a schoolchild had written to a friend: "Do you want to come over after school? Check yes or no"—with two little squares, neither checked.

My parents came into the kitchen, and I pulled them into the Display Room to show them the new items. Then we gathered around the stone table in the courtyard as I described spotting the paper inside the pipe at the market. They congratulated me again on my find, and we munched on cookies and drank lemonade. A beam of sunlight warmed my face, and I closed my eyes: I was happy here. I belonged here, at the museum with my family.

As I reached for one last cookie, I asked a question that had been on my mind since the market, since the man with the flannel vest wanted to show us a trick. "Why isn't magic allowed?"

My parents shifted in their seats, and Uncle Lem coughed; no one answered immediately.

"Do you know what magic is?" my father finally said.

I hesitated. No one at school or in town ever talked about magic, but I had read about it. Often it seemed silly, like making animals appear from oversized hats, or picking a certain coin from a pile. But the way my father said the word *magic*, it felt like something tangible, something powerful. Something that could lift me off my feet. I shook my head.

"Magic is everywhere," Uncle Lem said, pushing back his chair. "But only some can harness it properly." My parents looked at him quickly, but he went on. "There are different types of magic. One is the magic of illusion, where sleight of hand can fool the eye."

That was the magic I had read about, the kind the man at the market wanted to show us. "But there is another kind of magic," Uncle Lem said. "One that carries a powerful energy—that connects people, that can be manipulated, that can create. But magic of either kind has not been allowed for a long time."

"Why not?"

"People once could use magic freely, and they added goodness to the world. But some got greedy. They wanted to make more, to have more, and in the wrong hands that power hurt people and destroyed lands." I had learned about the wars in school. But they were about boundary disputes, not magic. At least, magic was never mentioned. "After the wars, magic was banned. Only certain people, mostly scholars, were allowed to know about it and study it," Uncle Lem said. "Everyone else was made to forget that magic could be manipulated, and eventually most forgot it ever existed."

"But why did they forget?"

"The magic relied on connections," Uncle Lem said, lifting a shoulder. "New technologies were developed that broke those connections. Instead of writing and receiving letters, people sent aer messages. Instead of cooking meals together, people started using food programmers. So the magic didn't have anything to hold on to."

"How do you know about magic? Were you one of those scholars?"

Uncle Lem laughed. "I'm not that old!" he said. "But if you look far enough back in our family tree, you'll find some of those scholars. And, as a child, I happened to be very fond of listening to bedtime stories."

"If magic needs objects that people share, like paper and books, wouldn't the museum be a perfect place for magic?"

Uncle Lem glanced at my parents. My father leaned forward to lift the lemonade pitcher and dipped his head at an angle so slight I couldn't tell if he was shaking it.

"Who wants a refill?" he said. "All this talk is making me thirsty." I held my glass out and watched as he poured the golden liquid into it.

"I think that's a long enough history lesson for today," Uncle Lem said, standing up.

My mother stood up, too, and pushed in her chair. "Do you want to read a little before we go?" she asked. I did, of course, and the grown-ups seemed like they had told me all they were going to for the moment. My mother went into the library with me to set up the book cradle, and rubbed her hand across my shoulders as the book opened.

"You'll like this one," she said. "There's a girl about your age who lives in a cottage in a city on the edge of an ocean. There's a shop in her neighborhood where they bake the most delicious desserts you could ever imagine—chocolate buns glazed with caramel, cupcakes topped with tiny marzipan deer and foxes that melt in your mouth. When you pull the door open and step inside, it's like walking through a cloud of spun sugar."

"You sound as if you've actually been there!" I said.

She smiled. "I'll let you read it for yourself."

But as much fun as it was to read, I wished she had told me more. I'd have given anything to hear her voice again.

On that wondrous day when I found my first paper, my mother had been afraid of losing me at the market—but it was my parents, two years later, who vanished.

CHAPTER
7

THE NEXT DAY, Uncle Renald gathered everyone in front of the library and gestured to Jane's stool, tucked against the wall. "I had been considering assigning more intellectually stimulating jobs today," he said. "But that will have to wait for another day." He assigned guarding duties again. Jane pursed her lips and Karl shuffled his feet, but Florence let out a loud sigh. Uncle Renald motioned for me to remove the stool. I had fetched the stool to help Jane, but instead it had caused trouble for all of them.

When I walked by later on feet made quiet with guilt, carrying a stack of napkins fresh from the laundry machine, I caught Karl fiddling with something in his hands. An aer reader? He spun it on his thumb like a regular ring and clamped his other hand over it as soon as he saw me.

But he'd turned over his aer reader the day the interns arrived, same as everyone else. Unless he managed to sneak it past Uncle Renald or got permission to keep it, but that seemed unlikely, especially when Uncle Renald had so adamantly refused to return the one I needed. Could it have been the museum's aer reader Karl was holding?

"Did my uncle give that to you?" I asked. "Is that the museum's aer reader?"

"What?" he said. "No." He twisted his hands, keeping the ring obscured.

I hated to think he was lying, but I hadn't noticed him wearing any jewelry earlier. If it was an aer reader, maybe I could use it to scan. Each aer reader was biometrically controlled, so if it wasn't the museum's it wouldn't work for me, but what if it was?

"Let me see it," I said. "Please."

He held up two empty hands.

"I know you had a ring." He stood up and turned out his pockets.

"Shake your leg," I demanded. He did. Nothing clattered to the floor.

Uncle Renald would have no reason to give him the museum's aer reader. And the last time Karl had his aer reader, it had been humming quietly, and I didn't hear anything like that now. Maybe

I was seeing things, but that wouldn't explain Karl's behavior. I arched an eyebrow at him and walked away to the library.

Hours later, while I was skimming a slim, green book about a boy chopping down a tree, a triangle of paper popped up in the crease between pages. I must have made a noise when I spotted it, because Florence stuck her head into the library from her guarding position. "Did you find something?" she asked.

"Yes!" I said. Florence looked left, then right, then bolted into the room. The paper was decorated with faint blue lines, and someone had drawn a hot-air balloon in pencil.

"What is it?" she asked.

"A bookmark," I said. "People put them in books to keep track of where they stopped reading." The books in the library were treasures, each one a door to a whole new world—but to find a connection to a real live person who had read this very same book before me felt colossal, whether it was a bookmark, a fossilized crumb stuck in the book's crease, or a thumbprint smudged on a page. "Some were designed specifically for readers to use as bookmarks, but a lot of the pieces I've found, like this one, seem to be random items people grabbed because they were nearby. I've found a ticket stub to a play, a flattened four-leaf clover, a grid that said BINGO on the top, and a card with a snow-covered dog wearing a pair of antlers."

Florence glanced at the paper triangle. "That's so interesting," she said, and went back to her spot outside the door.

I stared at the hot-air balloon, wondering who had drawn it and what their life had been like, what journey the slip of paper and the book had taken as they made their way to the Paper Museum.

Wanting to do one more book that day—I was desperately behind—I sent for the next one on the shelf. I was up to the authors whose last names started with *T*. This book was one I recognized, the one about the girl in the cottage and the bakery my mother loved. I flipped through it, remembering my mother's description of the bakery and its cloud of spun sugar. I was about to send the book back when a nearly invisible design—the same color as the page, since it was made *from* the page, the fibers of the papers pushed upward—stood out: an embossed circle with an open book inside it.

The sugar cloud in my head vanished. I had found the book. The one I had been looking for since my parents disappeared. The one that would show me how to get them back. Relief and joy rushed through me so quickly I felt light-headed.

But something was wrong. I was sure in the book I had seen in my mother's hands, the circle had been on a page with a black-and-white illustration. This page, and the one facing it, had nothing but words.

This wasn't the right book.

The cover of this book was plain brown; it was called *An Extraordinary Cottage by the Sea* and the author was Rayemor Tan. Nothing about the book seemed extraordinary. I examined the circle more closely: it was actually two separate circles, one on top of the other, the same pattern pressed into the book twice, almost exactly overlapping but with a fraction of one rim showing below the other. Had it been there when I'd read the book years before?

I sent it back and requested the next book. This one, too, I recognized. Even though I hadn't read it, my mother had described it to me vividly during one of my bedtime stories. *The Underwater Circus* by Eli Tanell. Holding my breath, I advanced the pages using the book cradle. From the bottom of a page about halfway through, a doubled circle stared up at me.

I should have been preparing supper, but instead I requested book after book. Many of the books by *T* authors had embossed circles. And they were all books that my mother had read, that she had told me stories from. I pored over each page that was marked. The stories didn't seem to have anything in common— they had different authors, different characters, different time periods. The one thing that was similar across the pages was a mention of water—a boat crossing an ocean, a character caught in a rainstorm, someone swimming in a lake. Was that significant? Why were the circles in those books? How did they get there? There could be dozens of books with a circle, maybe hundreds. There were thousands of books left and I would have to look at them all so carefully and, without the aer reader, so slowly. I tried not to think of the time I had lost by starting at the beginning, when the books with circles seemed to all be at the end. The right book was here somewhere, I knew it. But it was going to be much harder to find than I thought—it was as if I were in a field of grass looking for a flower, only to discover that each blade of grass had turned into a flower, too, and I had to find one particular bloom before they all wilted. A tear slipped from the corner of my eye, and I wiped at it with the base of my thumb before it could fall onto a page. Once, that page had been part of a living tree that relied on water to survive, but now a single drop could ruin it.

CHAPTER 8

I ROSE BEFORE DAWN the next morning with circles swirling in my head. It seemed almost impossible, but what if my mother had made the circles in the books? Maybe for some reason she had been marking ones she had read. Maybe Uncle Lem had given her an assignment. He kept a crate of tools in his book repair carrel, tucked into one of the library alcoves—I dressed quickly and headed over to check, spinning on a single lamp inside the dark library. The crate overflowed with brushes, clamps, and calipers. But there was nothing that would emboss a small circle shape onto a page.

Pink sunlight filtered through the windowpanes, and I wished I could stay within the grid of light and find the tool, find the book.

Find the arrow that pointed to my parents. My arms prickled with a twin hope and fear: hope that the right book would tell me where to find them, and fear that I wouldn't find them in time. I needed to confirm that the mayor's office had canceled the missing persons report. If Uncle Renald seemed to be in a good mood, I could ask again for the museum's aer reader. But I had another important task to complete before breakfast.

I hurried across the courtyard to Jane's quarters. It was her birthday, and I had made what we always used to make for each other's birthdays: a daisy chain to crown her head. Instead of giving it directly to her, I left it hanging on the doorknob outside her room. That way, if she didn't want to wear it, she wouldn't have to say so.

As I came out of the dormitory, a bird was trilling wildly, and Uncle Renald was bending below a sycamore tree at the far end of the courtyard. He scooped something up in a gentle gesture and, standing on tiptoes, deposited it into a nest on a low branch. As he backed away, a fledgling popped its head out of the small woven home, and the mother bird swooped to it, twittering. His kindness to the birds was encouraging—he did care for creatures other than himself. I moved toward him, hoping for a positive answer about the aer reader, but when he saw me coming, he scowled and stomped away.

At seven, when Jane walked into the courtyard with the daisy chain on her head, Uncle Renald curled his lip. Birthdays were special, and I didn't think even he could object to a simple embellishment for such an important day. His grumpiness did nothing to dampen my happiness that she'd accepted my gift.

Uncle Renald didn't assign guarding that day. Instead, he marched the interns to the library and allowed them to step in. I followed, thinking of the birthday cake that Jane's mother might send over. She often took the time to prepare food by hand instead of programming it, and her cakes tasted like they were made out of air and sugar.

Uncle Renald lectured for a long time on the importance of never touching anything in the library.

While he demonstrated how the book cradles worked, two things happened in such quick succession that they were almost simultaneous: a delivery box chirped outside the window, and Jane turned her head so fast that one of the petals from her daisy chain dislodged itself and spun away from her head. We watched as it floated down, landing firmly on the book displayed directly in front of Uncle Renald. Our heads swiveled as one to see his reaction. His face turned purple and splotchy, and he carefully plucked the petal with his padded fingers and held it in the air like a dead spider. "Everybody out," he said in a voice so quiet it felt dangerous.

We followed him to the courtyard. The delivery box chirped again and flew to Jane.

"Retrieve your parcel," Uncle Renald said, again in that low, controlled voice.

Jane, her hands shaking, took the delivery.

"Open it," he ordered.

She put the box on the ground and looked at the row of buttons on the front of the box. Blue to make the box transparent without opening it, silver to open it, and black to send it back. She pressed the silver button and the box unfolded and shrank into a flat disk, leaving a gorgeous-looking cake with frosted layers trimmed with apricots and blueberries.

"Today is your birthday?" he asked.

Jane nodded, staring at the cake. My mouth watered in spite of my apprehension.

"I was clear that nothing in the library was to be touched. Interns who break this rule have nothing to celebrate. It is no longer your birthday," he said, and we all gasped. He couldn't cancel a birthday!

But he had. Uncle Renald took Karl and Florence back into the library and allowed them to dust the backs of the chairs. He made Jane sit in the courtyard, fifty feet away from her cake, where she could see it but not eat it. I tried to sit with her, but he ordered me away. My legs felt hollow, as if I were made of sticks and held together by loose twine. A chipmunk ran up to the cake and grabbed a blueberry in its mouth, then ran away.

It was, of course, all my fault. If I hadn't made her the daisy chain, the petal wouldn't have landed on the book and she wouldn't have gotten in trouble and been denied her birthday cake. If I hadn't been at the museum, she wouldn't have come in the first place. For all the times she had treated me with kindness, I repaid her with punishment. I didn't deserve such a friend.

Daring to hope things could ever go back to the way they were before, even something as simple as making a daisy chain for a birthday, was like the last leaf clinging to a branch on a windy day, so easily snapped away and flung into the vast unknown. I needed to get away. For a while now, I hadn't allowed myself to go to the fort in the massive dogwood tree, a hideaway that had been a place of fun and a place of solitude, a place where Jane had sat by me for many hours after my parents' disappearance. But the tree was also where our friendship had splintered. It was beyond sight of the museum, tucked away in the woods, surrounded by tall oaks and pines and many years' worth of fallen leaves and needles. I never knew who built it or who else had played there, but Uncle Lem made it clear that it was mine. And it was where I needed to go.

I pushed aside the lower branches of the tree and stepped up to the wooden door carved into the trunk. It was stuck shut, and I gave it a shove with my shoulder. As it flung open, I fell into the fort and landed on the dirt floor. The familiar, earthy smell rushed to my nostrils, bringing a mix of memories of many happy hours spent here, as well as the ache of my later visits. My happiness and sadness had dwelled in here together, walled up in the dark tree. For a long time I lay on the floor, keeping still, trying not to feel.

When my body finally ached to move, I groped around for the portable light that hung near the door. I spun it on as I clambered to my feet.

A stream of light crossed at a low angle across the floor and highlighted a dangling cobweb. Shifting the light beam revealed a labyrinth of faded, stringy webs. I took the corner of my sweater and swiped at them furiously, slashing them into pieces. My sweater snagged on something on the wall, and when I pulled it loose, a circular groove sprang out from the bark. I pushed it back in place, and a small door opened in the wall, with a space behind it. In the space was a delivery box.

Uncle Renald's voice popped into my head: "Why don't you give it to her yourself?"

Had Uncle Lem left something for me?

The surface of the box was smooth and welcoming. As I reached out to press the OPEN button, my blood pounded rhythmically in my ears—*whoosh whoosh whoosh*—until the sound became almost deafening. The box unfolded, and sitting in its place was a green typewriter. Not one of the fourteen from the Typewriter Room. This was a fifteenth typewriter, completely different from any I'd seen before. And it was for me.

CHAPTER 9

THERE WAS A PIECE of paper loaded in the typewriter, left there as if someone had been called away in the middle of typing. I gingerly put my hand near the roller knob on the right side of the typewriter and was considering inching the paper up when I pulled back. Instead, I held the light beam above the typewriter and looked down so I could read the text. In dark ink it read:

```
When time is of the Essence, type what
you've always wanted to type:
```

The sentence ended not with a period but with a colon, inviting me to fill in the rest with my own words.

My fingers itched to type, but I was suddenly afraid of many things: afraid I wasn't allowed to touch the typewriter. Afraid to linger any longer in the dogwood fort in case Uncle Renald came looking for me. Afraid Jane was still sitting in the courtyard next to her cake. But I also wanted to stay, examining the typewriter until it grew dark outside and the birds began singing their night-time songs.

I would look at it for a minute, I told myself. In case there was a clue to my parents' whereabouts, or to where Uncle Lem had gone.

The typewriter was more square in shape than most of the ones in the museum, and its keys were silver circles. And the color! It was the green of cream of broccoli soup, the kind my mother used to make and I'd pretend to hate, though we both knew I loved it. I'd never seen a green typewriter, never imagined that one might exist.

I held my fingers above the keys, ran them in the air across the rows and down, back and forth, imagining how smooth they must feel. I counted the keys slowly: fifty. Twenty-six were letters, and, like the ones in the museum, they were not in alphabetical order, which I had never understood. The other keys were numbers, symbols, and function keys. Some of the symbol keys were archaic ones we didn't use anymore, such as # and &. I had always wondered what they meant, with their slanted lines and curves. It was strange to know that something that used to be important enough to be included on a typewriter was now useless, except as a pretty squiggle.

One letter key was missing from the keyboard, and I knew instantly from the location that it was the letter *L*. The one I most wanted to have there, since it was the first letter of my own name. The silver circle must have fallen off in the many years since the typewriter was made, but the nub underneath connected to the type bar—it might still type. Before I could lose my nerve, I put my finger on the *L* nub—it was colder than I expected—and pushed gently, not hard enough that it would reach the paper but enough to lift the metal spoke out from the fan of other letters and symbols. It rose into the air like a seesaw, hovering until I slowly took my finger off. It dropped back to its spot with the others.

As the spoke fell back into place, there was a sliding sound and a muted *thunk*, as though something leaning against the typewriter had slipped down. Running my hand around the side of the type-writer, my fingers found a small, flat object. When I pulled it closer and saw that it was an envelope, I let go as if it were on fire. There were no finger pads in the fort and my pockets were empty, so I had nothing to hold the envelope with. But if Uncle Lem had left it for me, surely I could touch it. I picked it up gently, the first time I had touched paper without wearing a finger pad. It was softer than I expected, and grainier, with horizontal ridges. My name was typed on the envelope, an island of black letters in the middle of a white sea. I carefully opened the flap. Inside was a square paper card.

The paper was as pristine as a freshly laundered sheet, but when I flipped it over, there was a message typed on the other side. It read:

> Neither snow, nor rain, nor heat, nor
> gloom of night stays these couriers from
> the swift completion of their appointed
> rounds.

It was a saying that my father and Uncle Lem had taught me, the unofficial motto of the messengers who used to deliver paper letters by hand. And, instantly, I was eight years old again, running through town with Jane. We were giggling, our feet slapping the cobblestone street as we tried to run without dropping the "letters" we had made of twigs, scraps of fabric, and dented cake pans. It was one of our favorite games, pretending to be messengers delivering letters through all types of weather, across all kinds of terrain.

Uncle Lem must have left the typewriter and this message to lift my spirits, to give me hope until he came back. Even though the envelope next to the typewriter had my name on it, I wanted to give the card to Jane to make up for ruining her birthday. A real delivery of an actual piece of paper.

The card fit into my back pocket without creasing, and I slid the envelope under the typewriter for safekeeping. As I searched for the groove to close the compartment, another object caught my eye—in the corner was a round tub, about the size of the inkwell in the Display Room. It was made out of a material I'd never seen before and, instead of having a TRANSPARENCY button, it had a cover that snapped on and off. When I popped the cover off, the sweet scent of almond paste floated out. Inside was a single marzipan butterfly, delicately crafted with pinks and greens and blues. It was hard and crumbling slightly around the edges. I put it in my sweater pocket.

My plan was to march straight to the courtyard, and, assuming Uncle Renald was not nearby, hand the piece of paper directly to Jane. On the walk back from the woods, I imagined her delight. "This is the best present anyone ever gave me!" she would say, and she would know how sorry I was about the cake.

About everything.

And we would be best friends again.

CHAPTER 10

I COULDN'T FIND JANE anywhere. Karl finally told me she hadn't been feeling well and Uncle Renald had given her permission to rest, so I peeked into the dormitory. She was curled into a ball with a blanket up to her chin—I didn't dare wake her. After propping the paper card on the cabinet next to her bed, I sneaked out. I wanted to be there when she first saw it, but it might be just as good to have her show it to me, and then I'd tell her it was from me.

When I emerged from the dormitory, a voice was calling from the front gate. A visitor? Uncle Renald strode across the court-yard, with Karl and Florence close behind. The museum was open to the public on Saturdays, from ten o'clock to noon. But today was Tuesday, and there was a man standing at the gate, looking as determined to visit the museum as Uncle Renald was to keep him out.

"I'm from the mayor's office," the man insisted. He was dressed in a light brown suit with a matching hat and had a briefcase at his feet. He took off his hat and wiped his brow, and I wondered what was in his briefcase. Most people used only aer readers to conduct business.

"We are not open to the public right now," Uncle Renald said, his arms crossed across his chest. "Come back on Saturday."

"I'm not the public," the man said. "Didn't you get an aer message that I was coming?" Uncle Renald said nothing, neither nodding nor shaking his head. "I'm from the mayor's office," the man said again. That seemed to be the only argument he had.

Was he coming to see me about the missing persons report? Or were we in trouble because I hadn't filed the bookmark report?

"Shouldn't you have a badge?" Florence said, from where she had stopped behind Uncle Renald.

"Ah, yes, of course," the man said, fiddling with his aer reader. An oversized projection named POSSIBLE SITES FOR NEW INITIATIVE came up, with three or four lines underneath, the text too small for me to read. "Pardon me," he said, then flicked his aer reader to show his badge with an insignia of the mayor's office. Droplets of sweat lined his forehead, and while Uncle Renald continued to stare in silence, the man placed his briefcase on the ground and popped open the lock. Inside was a single bottle of water, held in place with a thick strap. It seemed odd to bring a mostly empty case, unless he was planning on carrying something out of the museum. The man took the bottle out and gulped several large mouthfuls of water.

While he was drinking, Uncle Renald checked his aer reader. He did it quickly, barely dipping his head to look at his palm, and frowned before looking up. As the man put the half-empty bottle back in his briefcase, Uncle Renald plastered a fake grin on his face. "What exactly can I help you with?" he asked.

The man smiled and stepped forward. "I think we got off on the wrong foot," he said. "I'm here for a routine quality assurance check. Just need to verify that the museum is up to the proper standards of—" He paused and sniffed the air. "Quality."

"This is most unusual," Uncle Renald said, but he took the gate key from the depths of his pocket and unlocked the heavy front gate. "I can allow you twenty minutes." He turned toward the courtyard, and the man followed him, the rest of us trailing behind.

Outside the door to the Display Room, Uncle Renald informed the man that visitors were only allowed to glance into the rooms from the doorways unless they agreed to wear special magnetized gloves that would basically handcuff their hands while inside the rooms. He was serious about people not touching anything.

"I don't think those will be necessary," the man said, stepping into the room. Uncle Renald glared at him, but the man was careful not to touch anything, poking his head into every corner, nodding and making *hmm* noises to himself. Every once in a while he'd tap at his aer reader. When Uncle Renald cleared his throat, the man gave one last look at the room, eyes sweeping high and low, before he moved to the next room.

He went this way through every room, scanning, mumbling, taking notes. He said little, except to ask strange questions about a room's dimensions or ventilation system, as if he were looking for a spot where something could be hidden.

"I'm sure you found everything to be in order, then?" Uncle Renald said as they returned to the front door.

"Somewhat," the man said. "I'll need to check that building over there."

I glanced frantically across the courtyard—the dormitory was never shown to visitors! Jane would be mortified to be caught sleeping. And the paper! I shouldn't have left it out in plain sight!

"Well, be quick," Uncle Renald said. "You're about out of time." The man started to move toward the dormitory, but I moved in front of him so fast he almost tripped over me.

"One of the interns isn't feeling well," I said, trying to keep my words from racing into a jumble of sounds. "Maybe you could skip the dorm?"

"I need to see it," the man said, and moved around me.

Wake up, Jane, I thought. *Wake up and hide the paper.* In desperation, I whistled the birdcall we used to whistle back and forth to each other when we lived windows apart, the high-low *dee dee* copied from the chickadees that nested in our trees.

I whistled it again, louder. Halfway across the courtyard the man stopped and turned so abruptly I almost crashed into him.

"Are you whistling?" he said.

I clamped my lips together.

"Sounds like a black-capped chickadee, sir," Karl chimed in. "Pretty common around here."

"It's irritating," the man said. He adjusted his hat but resumed walking. I sent a silent *thank-you* to Karl.

As the man knocked on the door of the dormitory and then noisily turned the knob, I willed Jane to have heard my whistle and found the paper. She came out into the common room blinking, her door wide open behind her. The paper was on the cabinet. Uncle Renald and the man both looked at it at the same time. Uncle Renald jolted—a volcano bubbled beneath his skin, turning his face and hands a dark purple color—but he said nothing. I knew he was waiting for the man to leave before allowing his words to erupt.

The man stepped in and picked up the paper. "Very generous of you, Curator," he said, holding the card and turning to Uncle Renald. "Very generous indeed, allowing students to handle pieces of the collection. Clearly it's not that important to you." Uncle Renald snatched the paper, his face now splotched with patches of puce. Jane seemed equally upset by the presence of the man and the paper.

The man swung his gaze from Uncle Renald to Florence, who blinked twice in my direction and then straightened her glasses. "One final question," the man said. "Are there any storage closets in this dormitory?"

When the man had seen everything there was to see, he didn't look entirely happy. I wondered if we had failed the quality assurance check. While the man made notes on his aer reader, which he shook off and put back on several times, he looked in my direction more than once.

Did he suspect me of putting the paper there? Did he have information for me about the missing persons report? Uncle Renald opened the dormitory door, his lips pressed together, and everyone filed out. As I followed the man through the doorway, he stumbled, and his briefcase fell open at my feet. The bottle of water rolled out. I bent down and scooped it up, holding it out to him, torn between wanting to ask about the report and not wanting to get in trouble for the paper. The others were halfway across the courtyard. The question was on the tip of my tongue as he grabbed for the water bottle and leaned forward.

"Quick, tell me!" he demanded. "Where is it hidden?"

CHAPTER
11

I LET GO OF the water bottle and jumped back. Did he know about the typewriter in the fort?

"Where is it hidden?" the man repeated in an urgent whisper.

"Where is what hidden?" I asked, stalling. "What are you looking for?"

Uncle Renald paused on the other side of the courtyard and looked back at us. The man knelt and snapped the water bottle back into its spot in the briefcase, saying rapidly, "The foreign object that the mayor's office was informed of through the breach of protocol notification. Where are you keeping it?"

Did he mean the typewriter? "I have no idea what you're talking about," I told him. "I thought you were here to do a quality assurance inspection. I don't know anything about foreign objects."

"I happen to be conducting a little side business," the man said, showing his teeth through a narrow grin. "I also happen to be quite good at knowing when people are lying." He stood, holding his briefcase against his knee as he closed it.

"I'm not lying," I said.

The man ignored my comment. "According to the alert we received, the object was detected three months ago. It is potentially"—he dropped his voice—"*magical*, and therefore dangerous."

Three months ago. When my parents disappeared.

Magical?

The man went on in a low voice. "I knew the notification wasn't a glitch, no matter what the head curator said. If this object is what's causing the aer readers to slow down, and you can slip it to me, there will be a generous reward for both of us."

"What does this object look like?" I asked.

"That's what you're going to tell me," the man said.

By now Uncle Renald had turned around and was heading back toward us.

"I haven't seen a foreign object, honestly. But there is something I need to ask you." I hurried on before he could stop me. "I filed a missing persons report for my parents, but it was a mistake.

I didn't realize it would delete their accounts and housing if they weren't found soon. I tried to deactivate the report, but I'm not sure if it worked. Could you check?"

His eyes narrowed. But he turned on his aer reader and tapped a few times. "You're right," he said. "There's been a mistake." Relief flooded through me, until he kept talking. "Looks here like your parents are listed as partial owners of this museum, and since the main owner"—he looked to the side as if Uncle Lem would materialize next to him—"is also absent, the report should also have indicated that if they do not activate their aer readers within the given time frame, the museum will be reassigned too."

"You can't do that!" I cried. "My family has run this museum for generations."

"We're going to shut down your antiquated little institution either way," he said, snapping his palm closed. "As soon as we have a valid reason to overrule the jurisdiction restriction. Maybe if you turn over that foreign object, I could see about slowing things down a bit."

"I don't have a foreign object. I don't even know what it is! And you can't shut the museum down—it's too valuable! If more people came here, they would know that." In desperation I added, "What happened to the marketing plan for getting more people to come?"

"More visitors?" The man took off his hat and fanned himself with it. "A very interesting idea."

I didn't like the way he said that.

Uncle Renald finally reached us. "You've overstayed your welcome," he said to the man.

"You'll be hearing from my office," the man said to Uncle Renald, patting his briefcase. He turned to me, his upper lip hooked in a snarl. "Make sure to report any interesting finds immediately."

Uncle Renald crossed his arms and walked the man out.

"He's threatening to close the museum," I said. "To reassign it." I couldn't bring myself to mention my role in that threat, but I wasn't sure he even heard me. The purpleness of his face had barely subsided, and he hitched his head in the direction of the museum, where Jane, Florence, and Karl waited.

The mayor's office couldn't reassign the museum. And what foreign object could the man have been talking about? Uncle Lem hadn't gotten any new items in the past three months—I knew every inch of the display cases. Could it have been the typewriter? And was it a coincidence that the object supposedly appeared three months ago, the same time my parents disappeared? What did the man mean when he said it was magical? Could it—

"Someone has made a grave error in judgment," Uncle Renald said, slicing through my thoughts. He pulled Jane's paper from his pocket. "How did you get this?" he asked her. I swallowed hard and forced myself not to look at my feet.

"I've never seen it before," Jane said.

Uncle Renald snorted, then beckoned with his long pointer finger, and the four of us followed him, single file, into the museum, stopping in front of the Mechanical Devices Room.

"Which one of you miscreants had the audacity to use one of the museum's typewriters?" he said, his gaze shifting to each of us in turn, lingering on me. None of us answered.

Because the truth was, none of us had used the museum's typewriter. But I could not tell Uncle Renald that without telling him where the card came from, and that was not information I wanted to share.

He pushed the door open and made a great show of leading us to the rows of typewriters in the back room. He moved methodically from one to the next, inspecting each one. It was clear, even from the doorway, that none had been touched. The same pieces of paper, *The quick brown fox jumps over the lazy dog*, were centered exactly where they had always been.

Uncle Renald either couldn't tell they hadn't been touched, or he was pretending. He took a white handkerchief from his pocket and handed it to me, indicating I should dab it against the ink roller on each typewriter. I held up the handkerchief after each dab for his inspection. No black smudges.

He crooked his finger and we followed again, this time to the Display Room. Florence went first. She stood right behind him as he made a point of opening each case and counting every item to make sure nothing was missing. Everything was in its place.

"Who was assigned to guard this room today?" he asked. We looked at one another in confusion.

"No one, sir," Karl said. "You didn't assign anyone today."

"Outside," Uncle Renald said, and his voice was like a rock teetering on the edge of a cliff. We turned and walked back to the courtyard. He led us to the front gate, to a scraggly patch of dirt that used to have flowers growing in it.

"Paper is not for personal use," Uncle Renald said. He held up the square of paper, angled so it was facing us but he could still read it. "Neither snow, nor rain, nor heat, nor gloom of night," he read, and I struggled not to look at Jane at the sound of the familiar words, "stays these couriers from the swift completion of their appointed rounds."

He pointed at the ground. "Each of you find a stick." Karl grabbed one for each of us from under a nearby oak tree. "Write this in the dirt: I WILL NOT WASTE PAPER. Write it until the sun sets, and then you may go to bed."

It was humiliating, writing in the dirt with a stick. Jane, Karl, and I started scratching letters. Florence stood there, poking at her shoe with her stick.

"What are you waiting for?" Uncle Renald demanded of Florence. She rubbed her nose, knocking her glasses askance.

"We weren't taught writing at my school," she said. "It's kind of . . . old-fashioned."

It was true. No one really wrote anymore. Aer readers required recognizing the letters but not writing them, although some models offered a finger-stylus feature. I hadn't realized that some schools had stopped teaching writing altogether, though. It seemed like something people should know.

Uncle Renald was relentless. "Then you can wipe the letters away when the dirt is full," he said, turning back to the museum, "so the others can keep writing."

We wrote it over and over.

I WILL NOT WASTE PAPER.

I WILL NOT WASTE PAPER.

I WILL NOT WASTE PAPER.

The sun moved across the sky.

I stood between Jane and Karl, while Florence was stationed at the other end of the dirt patch, ready with a tree branch to sweep out our letters when we ran out of room. Every so often a breeze kicked up and scattered fallen leaves across our writing area. Florence cleared them away. Our fingers grew numb. It was past suppertime—my stomach was empty. We said nothing, afraid Uncle Renald would materialize out of thin air and punish us more. Finally, I risked a glance at Jane.

"I'm sorry," I said. "This must be the worst birthday in history."

She looked over at me and smiled. I didn't know how she could still smile. "It's not my birthday anymore, remember?"

And then it struck me how much I disliked Uncle Renald. He had no right to treat others like this. I wanted Uncle Lem back. *I want my parents back*, I thought, and the force of it stung. "Good thing," I said. "Because this would be a rotten one."

We returned to our writing, but I could focus on nothing except getting my parents—and Uncle Lem—back. I stretched my stick out a little farther, to the spot where Karl was writing. "NEED YOUR HELP," I scratched. When he looked up, I wrote: "AER READER." His face froze for an instant, then he started to write back, but the sound of approaching footsteps crunched. He hurriedly stubbed out the messages with his boot before Uncle Renald got closer, but the steps weren't coming from the direction of the museum. Someone was approaching from outside the gate.

A clean-cut man dressed in a black suit came into view. Florence was closest to the gate and he tipped his hat at her, then stared at the rest of us before flashing on his aer reader to display a badge. It had the same insignia of the mayor's office that the earlier visitor had shown. "Can you fetch the curator, please?" he asked. "I'm here for a brief inspection. I believe he's expecting me."

CHAPTER 12

UNCLE RENALD WAS QUITE RUDE. He called the man a fraud and said the mayor's office was inept, sending two inspectors in one day, but, as Uncle Renald ranted, the man simply made a note in his aer reader, tipped his hat, and left.

After the man departed, Uncle Renald examined our scratches in the dirt. He gave a quick flick of his hand, which seemed to mean he was disgusted with everything and we should all go to the dormitory for the night. My stomach growled on the way back; Jane's did too.

"Why would the mayor's office send two men?" Jane asked, when the four of us were sitting around the table in the common room.

"Florence?" I said.

She looked at me quickly. "How should I know?"

"That man seemed to recognize you. Maybe the first one did too."

She didn't answer. Karl's stomach rumbled now, and he stood up and went over to his room. Leaving his door open, he rummaged through the trunk at the end of his bed.

"Do you know them?" Jane asked. She asked in a gentle voice, but I could tell she was more than curious.

"Maybe they've seen me," she said. "I've been to city hall before. Civics study."

"They'd remember you from that?"

Florence slid her finger back and forth against the edge of the table. We waited. Then she added, "Well, or it could be because my father works in city hall."

"Why didn't you say so?" Jane said. "What does he do there?"

Florence shrugged, her eyes on the floor. Then she said, "Cleans up messes."

Why was she ashamed that her father was on the sanitation crew? I wouldn't care. I would never be embarrassed about my father.

"So you live in the city?" I asked.

"Yes," she said.

I'd been to the city a couple of times—it was flat and grid-like: smooth roads laid out in straight lines, buildings all the same height and painted the same color. The town was built on a hill, with winding streets and arches. Most of the houses, while they were made of the same kind of stone, had their own character, and were decorated with designs and flowers that indicated who lived there. The city felt like the set of paper dolls in the museum's display case. But taking the transport cube to get there was fun, as was walking under the giant aer reader screens that projected advertisements for fancy shoes and warm pretzels and blasted out music or a salty, doughy smell to tempt people's appetites.

Karl came back to the table with a handful of granola bars. "Anyone else hungry?" he said.

"Starved!" Jane said, reaching for one. "Thanks."

"Do you live in the city too?" I asked Karl.

"What? Yes." He seemed startled at my question, but maybe he hadn't heard the conversation with Florence.

We each ate a granola bar, but I was still hungry. Across the courtyard in the museum, all the windows were dark. Uncle Renald had gone to bed early again. "I'm going to get more food," I said.

"Are we allowed to?" Jane asked.

"I'm too hungry to sleep," I said. "Karl, will you come with me?"

He slowly got to his feet.

In the kitchen, I programmed a chicken potpie large enough for all of us. I gathered plates and forks while the red lights of the food unit ticked down the minutes. Karl poked around silently in the cabinets.

"I'll cut to the chase," I said. "I need to borrow the aer reader."

He jammed his hands into his pockets. "Even if I have one," he said, his voice low, "this isn't the best time."

"Better to give it to me than have Curator Renald find out about it," I said.

That made him pause. "What do you need it for?"

"To send a message and check on a report." I didn't mention it was a missing persons report. "And to scan books in the library. For a project I'm working on."

He pulled his hand out of his pocket with the aer reader on his thumb. He slowly twisted it off.

"Thank you," I said, reaching for it. "Is this the museum's aer reader? Did Uncle Renald give it to you?"

"No," he said. "I have two models. I gave one back to my parents and kept the other."

If it wasn't the museum's aer reader, it wouldn't work for me. But I didn't entirely believe him when he said it wasn't—why would he have two models? I put the aer reader on my thumb. As soon as it slid on, however, the image projected on my palm reverted to the welcome page, blinking Karl's name. It wasn't the museum's, so it wouldn't accept my prints, and I wouldn't be able to use it. My fingers prickled with disappointment.

"It's not working?" he said, the expression on his face an odd combination of unease and relief.

"No," I said. "Can you add me as a guest?" I wasn't sure that was possible, but it was worth asking.

Karl hesitated. When the screen powered up instantaneously for him, he shook his free hand nervously, then pasted a smile on his face and played with the settings. "Try that," he said, but it still didn't work for me. Maybe he could check the report for me. And maybe I could convince him to scan books for me. But I didn't think Uncle Renald would allow that, and, anyway, I needed to make sure it was done right. I needed to find the book myself.

"Can you send a message for me?" I asked. He clicked to his inbox. I gave him the message address for Uncle Lem. I didn't expect Uncle Lem to tell me where he was, if he couldn't, but maybe he could say he was okay or when he'd be back. I tried not to think of Uncle Renald's remark—*if* Uncle Lem came back.

I leaned closer to make sure Karl entered the address correctly, and as Karl started to fill in Uncle Lem's name, the autofill kicked in and finished it. Why would Karl's aer reader have Uncle Lem stored as a contact?

For a fraction of a second I wondered if there was something going on that I didn't know about. But, of course, Uncle Lem was stored as a contact because he was in touch with all the interns when they initially applied for the session. Before he left.

"Tell him that I need him home, please, as soon as he can. Ask him if he knows anything about a foreign object. And sign it *Lydia*."

Karl's fingers paused in midair. "A foreign object?"

It was possible he asked simply out of curiosity, but after my encounter with the man from the mayor's office earlier, I was not in a trusting mood. "What do you know about it?"

"Nothing," he said quickly. "Nothing at all."

"Send the message, please."

Karl did as I asked.

Next I directed him to the missing persons page. He couldn't access the full report, but the public view was detailed enough to show that not only was it still active, but a picture of the museum now floated below the picture of my parents' house in town.

The staccato tone of the timer for the chicken potpie filled the air, and I silenced it. Karl put his aer reader back in his pocket and got a tray to carry the potpie on while I went to the linen cabinet for napkins. I grabbed the pile of plates and forks as we headed out the door.

The pie was hot, but tasted bland. Jane stabbed at chunks of carrot and moved them around on her plate.

"Not as good as your mom's, I know," I said. She smiled at me, but it was a small smile. I tried a bite of the doughy crust. "I bet you'll be glad to go home for a bit before you start your next internship." I tried not to think that I might not have a home when that time came. And I hoped she wouldn't want to leave early, after her ruined birthday and Uncle Renald's meanness.

She speared a rectangle of potato. "I'm not sure I'm doing another internship."

"What else would you do?" She and her mom had always talked about opening a bakery together and making all sorts of tiny, delicious desserts, as they called them. Like the butterfly in my pocket. But her mom still worked at the spice terminal, as far as I knew.

"Grandma Hastings," she said.

"No," I said, but Jane nodded.

"She needs help with the shop, even though she keeps insisting she doesn't." Jane's grandmother ran a trinket shop in a town to the north. She collected and sold every sort of gadget—some broken, some not. But mostly broken. I don't know how she stayed in business.

"What kind of shop?" asked Karl. I hadn't realized he'd been listening to our conversation.

"A run-down one," Jane said. "She fixes junk and sells it."

"That sounds fun!" said Karl.

"If you like not making any money and living up north."

"Your brother can't go?" I asked.

"He's already been accepted for law study." She speared another potato on top of the one already on her fork.

"Can't she close the shop and move in with your family?"

"You know she won't," Jane said, finally eating the potato pieces.

I tried to picture Jane in a dusty old shop, rusty metal coils springing off the shelves. She'd be wearing a clean white apron with a zinnia embroidered on it.

"Is there any way out of it?" I asked. "It's so far away."

"We can't leave her up there alone," Jane said. "I don't know how soon she'll need me, but when she does, I'll go." Family didn't leave family—not if they had a choice. The rest of the pot-pie on my plate was now cold.

Jane put her fork down and leaned close to me. "Thank you for the birthday message," she whispered.

I was at once delighted that she recognized it for what it was and mortified at how the situation had turned out.

"Come outside with me," I told her. "I have one last birthday present for you. Something you can keep this time."

Jane helped me gather the plates and forks and napkins onto the tray and followed me outside, where the moon was almost full. I put the tray on the ground and gave her the tub from my pocket.

"It's too beautiful to eat!" she said, when she opened it. "Almost. Actually, we better eat it right away." She broke the butterfly in two and handed half to me.

"Jane," I said, holding the piece carefully between my finger and thumb. "I'm so sorry. About the day you left. I'm sorry I yelled at you. I didn't know what I was saying."

Her lips quivered. "I thought you hated me," she said.

"I didn't. I don't." I said. "I never could."

"You're my best friend," she said. "And I know your parents being missing is not easy. I get that you need to be alone sometimes." She laughed. "Just tell me in a nicer way next time!" She held up her butterfly half and popped it into her mouth.

The piece she gave me looked like a corner taken from a stained-glass window.

It tasted like swirled sweetness from a faraway world.

"Happy birthday," I said.

The moon was high above the courtyard as I crossed back again to the kitchen to drop off the dirty dishes. My heart was renewed by Jane's confirmation that we were friends, but my head churned with thoughts of my house and the museum being reassigned, a foreign object that might have had something to do with my parents' disappearance, and the typewriter in the dogwood fort with the message. I needed more answers.

If Uncle Lem had found a foreign object, where would he have put it? I knew the museum forward and backward but did a sweep of the display cases and storage rooms just in case, spinning on a hand lantern instead of the overhead lights even though Uncle Renald was in bed. As expected, nothing was out of the ordinary. Maybe I could find a way to check Uncle Lem's room, but now that Uncle Renald was in there, that would be more difficult.

The only new item I'd come across was the typewriter, and that was about as foreign as my own hand. Unless the word *foreign* meant something different than I thought.

Putting the hand lantern on the library table, I sent the book handler for a book that had long fascinated me, one my parents had taught me could be a valuable tool: *Merriam-Webster's Collegiate Dictionary, Eleventh Edition*. It described what a countless number of words meant, including old-fashioned ones that were not used anymore. There were multiple definitions for *foreign*, but all along the lines of what I thought: "something from outside, relating to a person or thing other than the one under consideration, not related or connected to a place." I hadn't come across any objects like that at the museum.

I flipped the dictionary to the *E* section. *When time is of the Essence, type what you've always wanted to type.* Several of the entries for *essence* stood out:

"The most significant element, quality, or aspect of a thing or person; 'in essence'—in or by its very nature; 'of the essence'—of the utmost importance."

None of the definitions described *essence* with an uppercase *E*. I wasn't sure how much this information helped. *Type what you've always wanted to type*—at least I knew what that was. I pictured the room full of typewriters, the same sentence typed over and over. But was I really supposed to type it myself? And when?

I sent the dictionary back and spun off the lamp. As I sneaked down the hall past Uncle Renald's room, a creaking noise startled me. I turned quickly, but his door was closed, and for a second a dark blue glow flashed on the threshold. When I blinked it was gone, and I rubbed my hands across my eyes, unsure if I could handle any more strangeness from this long day.

CHAPTER
13

MY PARENTS DISAPPEARED ON a beautiful spring day with not a hint of cloud in the sky, just as there was no trace of where they had gone. I was supposed to be staying after school with Jane for knitting club, but at recess I discovered I had only one of my needles. So, instead, I stopped by my parents' work building—I wanted to tell them how well I'd done on a test. My father was a data analyst at the Science Commission, and my mother was a laboratory officer. I loved sitting at my father's desk and watching number projections fly through the air on the wall and seeing my mother in her long apron and goggles moving from one station to another, checking on her projects and her colleagues. But they weren't at their work building.

"They left a couple of hours ago," one of the front door guards told me.

There was no sign of them at home, so I took the path to the museum.

I had my own key to the gate, but the front door was locked. It was never locked. "Hello?" I called, banging on the heavy front door. It opened when I was mid-knock, and I almost tumbled into Uncle Lem.

"Lydia, what a surprise!" he said, glancing down the hallway behind him. "How are you?" But before I could answer, he continued, "Would you like some refreshments? Go sit in the courtyard and I'll bring some out."

"Thank you," I said. "But I'm looking for my parents. Are they here?"

"Are they here?" Uncle Lem repeated.

A crash sounded from inside his room, followed by a tinkling sound like breaking glass. "I'll be right back," he said, closing the door firmly but leaving it unlocked.

I waited outside for a minute before I opened the door and peeked in. Uncle Lem was probably in the kitchen getting the refreshments he'd offered, so I poked around the rest of the museum. The Display Room was empty, as was the Mechanical

Devices Room. I found my mother in the library, and what she was doing sent a ripple of shock through me. She was reaching for a book in the book handler without wearing finger pads. She picked up the book with her bare hands and held it to the window, tilting it left and right. There was a picture on the page that looked like a crowd of people drawn in black and white, and when the sunlight streamed through the window directly to the bottom of the page, it lit up a mark that was otherwise almost invisible: a circle with a book in it.

"Mother!" I said, and at the sound of my voice she snapped the book shut.

"Sweetie!" she said, and in her tone there was a sense of urgency. "I thought you were at knitting club?"

"I lost one of my needles," I said. "Again."

"Oh, Lydia," she said. "Check the hall closet at home. If you run along now, you should be able to catch the tail end of your meeting."

Just then my father walked in carrying a tray of clear vials filled with brightly colored liquids—oranges and blues—as well as the silver triangular one from the Old and Useless Things Market. He said, "The mixing bottle—" but broke off when he saw me.

"Father?" I said. He put the tray down as quickly as my mother had closed the book. The tray also held a metal tool I didn't recognize and a plasticress box the size of a thimble—something fluttered inside it. My father covered it deftly with his hand.

"Aren't you supposed to be doing something this afternoon?" he asked.

They were definitely trying to get rid of me. "I got a good score on my geometry test today," I said, a little miffed. "I wanted to tell you."

My mother came over and hurriedly kissed me on the forehead, while my father said, "That's great, honey!"

"What are you two doing in here?" I asked.

"We're finishing up a repair job with one of the books," my father said.

"Shouldn't Uncle Lem do that?"

"This is one your father and I are helping with," my mother said. "We should be done in an hour or so."

My father added, "We'll be home by supper, and afterward we can go out for ice cream to celebrate your good grade!"

They hurried me out before I could ask more questions. I found the needle, met up with Jane, and brought home a slightly crooked basket-weave square to show them at supper.

Except they didn't make it home for supper. I ran to the museum, but they weren't there, and neither was Uncle Lem.

I ran to Jane's house, and her mother called my parents' work building in case they'd gone back there, but there was no sign of them. "Did they mention that they were going somewhere?" she asked. "Maybe they told you and you forgot? Have they been acting strange at all?"

They had practically shoved me out of the museum, something they had never done before—but it wasn't *that* strange. Not strange enough that they'd leave without telling me. "No," I said. "Nothing like that."

Jane said I could stay with her, but I wanted to check the museum again. Uncle Lem was back, planting flowers around the edge of the courtyard. He looked surprised to see me, and more surprised to learn that my parents couldn't be found. "I thought they'd gone home while I popped over to city hall and the garden shop," he said.

"They're not anywhere!" I said, my voice reaching a pitch so high and thin it could snap in two.

We checked the library, since it was the last place I'd seen them. The tray my father had put on the table was there, but it was empty. Nothing else looked out of place, although Uncle Lem picked up a piece of broken glass. The book handler was in its original position, waiting to fetch a book. If they had left a book out, after five minutes of inactivity the book handler would have reset itself, sending back whatever book it was holding.

We checked the other rooms. Uncle Lem even checked his own room. They weren't at the museum.

"Something must have gone wrong," Uncle Lem said to himself, but I heard it.

"Are they okay?" I asked, desperate for him to say yes.

But instead he said, "We'll find them, Lydia. We need to be patient."

"Should we report them missing with city hall?" I asked.

"No," he said too quickly. "But maybe we should check with the hospital in case one of them got hurt and had to rush off." But I could tell he didn't think that was the case.

They weren't at the hospital. I made Uncle Lem take me to every place in town that sold ice cream in case they'd stopped on the way home and gotten stuck somewhere. Nothing. No one had seen them. They had simply vanished.

My mother's words from that day at the Old and Useless Things Market, which now seemed like a lifetime ago, echoed in my head: *If we get separated, wait for us at the museum.* I moved in with Uncle Lem at the museum that same night. He insisted I finish the remaining weeks of school and encouraged me to go each day, but I couldn't concentrate at all. Each morning I ran back to our house in town, where I had left the front light on in case they came home in the dark, but the light was silently spinning its beam, standing watch over an empty house. As soon as school was done for the day, I ran to their work building, to the park, to the river, anywhere they might have gone. I asked their coworkers and my neighbors and the shopkeepers over and over if they'd seen my parents, so many times that they started shaking their heads *No, sorry* when they saw me coming. So I went back to the museum and waited.

CHAPTER
14

SOMETIMES I HEARD MY parents whispering my name, but when I turned, there'd be no one behind me. Sometimes, before I woke up in the morning, I smelled coffee and heard their footsteps criss-crossing the hall outside my room.

But after the visits from the mayor's office, the steps of strangers echoed in my sleep, brought on by the way the first inspector had responded to my suggestion of bringing more visitors to the museum, and reminding me that if my parents weren't found in time, a whole new family could be living and working at the Paper Museum. The footsteps reverberated in my head even after I woke up the following Saturday morning, so loud I couldn't shake them away. The sounds were real. I dressed at top speed and ran across the courtyard and down the path: there were at least fifty people milling around by the front gate. They looked like a sea of colored laundry. The air smelled of the dirt churned up by their feet.

"We're here for the open house!" announced a man wearing a hat shaped like a turtle.

A woman with hair longer than I'd ever seen stood near him. She waved her hand through the gate and bent down slightly to make eye contact with me. "Let us in, dearie, would you?" The crowd of people behind her pushed and pulsed.

"There is no open house," I stammered. "It's not even visiting hours yet. Not until ten o'clock. You're too early."

A woman thrust her palm in my direction and showed me her aer reader projection.

OPEN HOUSE AT THE PAPER MUSEUM, it blinked in big letters across the top. COME EARLY TO PREVIEW ITEMS. BOOKS! PRIZES! UPGRADES!

"Wait . . . please," I said, and ran back to the courtyard, where Uncle Renald and the interns were coming out the front door, their ears tilted toward the gate.

"There's a mob of people out front," I panted.

"Today you will wash windows," Uncle Renald said, handing a rag to each of the interns and then one to me.

I took it, not sure why he wasn't doing anything about the people at the gate. "They said they're here for an open house. Are we having an open house?"

"No, we are not." He held up a rag, roughly square in shape. "I assume this is another dim-witted ploy of the mayor's to make us look bad," he said, his voice rising a notch with each syllable, "when, in fact, it is his office that is foolish! Now *focus*. This is how to fold the rag for washing." I clenched mine into a ball instead.

Uncle Renald handed out buckets. As he gave me one, he asked, "How many people are there?"

"I couldn't count them all. At least fifty."

A crease appeared on his forehead, but Uncle Renald said nothing. Karl spoke up instead. "Did they say what they want?"

"They want to come in," I said.

Jane twisted her rag between her hands. Florence dumped her rag into her bucket.

"They can't," Uncle Renald said. "Not until ten o'clock. At which point you will cease washing windows and resume your guarding duties. No one is to go near the front gate." He hurried into the museum, calling out, "Fill your buckets and get started!" Through the window by the outdoor faucet, I watched him move down the hallway until he reached his room. When he opened the door, the wall panel flashed into sight—full of knobs and buttons. The one time I had asked Uncle Lem about them, he had waved his hand and said, "Security, hot air, cold air—I'll explain them all in due time." But that time hadn't come yet. If only there was a button that would restore everything to the way it used to be.

As the morning wore on, the sounds from the front increased. Peeking from the far edge of the courtyard, I could see there were more people at the gate now, maybe close to a hundred. Once in a while someone would shout something, but it didn't sound entirely unfriendly. Were all these people really interested in seeing the museum? I wondered if Uncle Renald would want me to lead a tour—a thought equally terrifying and thrilling.

I washed windows as quickly as possible, my arms scrubbing steadily in wide circles, pausing only to dip the rag in the bucket. With each swipe of the rag, I pushed aside thoughts of the people at the gate and focused instead on my parents. I needed to find the book my mother had been holding. I also needed to check Uncle Lem's room for a possible foreign object—or maybe he'd hidden it in the dogwood fort and I'd missed it?

Without noticing, I had moved away from the others as I worked. When I approached a window near the library, voices caught my attention—Karl and Uncle Renald were arguing inside. I stopped scrubbing and put my ear to the glass in time to hear Uncle Renald say, "No. End of discussion." His footsteps pounded down the hallway.

A minute later Karl emerged from the front door, a dark look on his face. "Did you hear back from Uncle Lem on the aer reader?" I asked.

"No," he said. I dropped my rag into my bucket, ready to interrogate further, but the clock struck ten and Uncle Renald marched out the door and pointed at me.

"Follow me." I straightened up immediately. Uncle Renald told Karl, Jane, and Florence to station themselves at their assigned doors, and they disappeared inside. The crowd at the gate maintained a low rumble. I tried to picture two hundred feet filling the empty courtyard, but it felt impossibly out of place.

The crowd quieted as Uncle Renald approached. "Visiting hours will begin now," he said. "One visitor is permitted at a time, for ten minutes each." A shout of protest came up from everyone but the man wearing the turtle hat, who was first in line. As Uncle Renald began unlocking the gate, they began jostling one another, pushing shoulders and elbows. Uncle Renald's hand froze in midair, the key not yet turned in the lock. "If there is fighting of any kind, no one will be allowed in."

The crowd groaned but backed off. The man in the turtle hat bounded along the path.

"Hurry up!" someone shouted from behind us as we walked toward the courtyard.

The man stopped to take in the courtyard, the museum, and the dormitory building. Perhaps he also noticed the bed of marigolds arrayed along the stone wall, or the grassy field that led off to the far woods, but if so he did not look at them long.

"Where do we start?" the man asked, pushing open the front door. "What do you have here anyway?"

Uncle Renald didn't blink. "Visiting is restricted to the library, the Display Room, and the Mechanical Devices Room. Touching is forbidden." He held out a pair of the special magnetized gloves for visitors.

The man complained the whole time, but allowed Uncle Renald to put the gloves on him. They snapped into place at his wrists, instantly pulling his hands together in front of his stomach. Uncle Renald gestured toward the library, which Florence was guarding, and the man walked in, his head moving from side to side as he scanned the shelves of books. I tried to point out some of the better-known titles, but he spun to the next room. He spent exactly two minutes in each room, swiveling his head so fast I was sure he would get a headache.

"Can I put my name down for one of the display cases, when it's empty?" he asked.

"Excuse me?" Uncle Renald said.

"I could use it for my shop. The flyer mentioned this was a preview for the upcoming estate sale."

"My job as curator is to keep the collection intact, not to parcel it out, no matter what the *flyer* may say. So, no, you may not put your name down for anything."

"Fine," the man said. "I'm really here for the new aer reader model giveaway. My reader is blipping all the time. Do I get that on the way out, or do I have to fill out the customer experience survey first?"

These people weren't here to see the museum. They thought they were getting upgraded aer readers! And how could they think they could *buy* items from our collection? I couldn't even fathom the display cases being opened and our cherished artifacts being dispersed among strangers who didn't know or even care about their history, who would probably use a stapler as a doorstop or a paper straw as a cat toy.

Uncle Renald said nothing. He marched the man back to the front gate before taking off the gloves.

"Is there an aer code for the survey I fill out?" the man said. "I could use that upgrade."

The lady with the long hair put her hands out sweetly as she pushed her way through the gate. "My turn," she said.

"Hey!" the man shouted, his face as red as a tomato. "You didn't answer me!" I ran to catch up to Uncle Renald and the lady, who were already walking toward the museum. She chatted as we walked, addressing most of her comments to me. "Must be lovely to live here," she said. I looked at Uncle Renald before answering, but he stared straight ahead.

"Yes," I agreed, thinking of Uncle Lem.

"It's so peaceful here! Not like town nowadays. Everyone in a rush, complaining about aer readers, angry with shopkeepers, pushing each other in the streets."

"Pushing each other?" I said.

But she ignored me. "There must be so many unique items here," she went on, and when I hesitated, thinking that she wanted some for herself, she added, "Valuable items?"

Uncle Renald rolled his eyes and flipped the hood of his long vest over his head.

"Only if you like paper, ma'am," I said.

Inside the museum, she spent her entire ten-minute allotment in front of the Golden Books section in the library, and then politely asked for one with a red-and-blue tugboat on the cover. How could people think it was okay to take items from the museum? Didn't they realize it was a collection, our livelihood, years and years of gathering and caretaking? The lady's cheerful face turned pouty when Uncle Renald said no. "But it'll go perfectly with my new bathroom drapes!" she said. "The flyer said to ask for a free book!"

Back at the front gate, the lady announced, "He didn't even give me a *book*." A low grumble started from the group.

Someone from the back shouted, "What about the aer readers?" Another voice called, "Skip the tour—give us aer readers!" and another, "This is going to take forever!" I'd never seen people behave like this. The man in the turtle hat had said his aer reader was behaving strangely, but after watching these people at the gate, it seemed clear *they* were the ones acting up.

A shoe came flying from the back of the crowd and bounced off the gate. "Give us aer readers!" several voices shouted together.

In a voice as short as a mowed lawn, Uncle Renald said, "Visiting hours will end at noon." It must have taken the crowd a few seconds to realize that the vast majority of them would not be getting in today, and would therefore definitely not be getting an aer reader, because two seconds later there was a low roar and the crowd surged forward, pushing through the gate. A large man plowed into Uncle Renald, knocking him to the ground, and someone bumped me into the hydrangea bush on the side of the path. The herd stampeded toward the courtyard. I pulled myself out of the bush, Uncle Renald scrambled to his feet, and we ran after them.

Two hundred feet pounding through the courtyard sounded completely wrong. The sound of them tearing open the front door and moving as a mass into the museum was worse. Uncle Renald ran straight into his room, moving faster than I have ever seen him move, while the man in the turtle hat and the lady with long hair led the crowd into the library. Attempting to guard the rooms was useless, so Jane and Karl ran after them, followed closely by Florence. There were too many people. They were reaching for books, pulling them off the shelves, and tossing them to the ground before reaching for more.

"Stop!" I shouted, but nobody listened. I grabbed the arm of the person nearest me and yanked on it, but they shook me off.

People were flinging books with abandon. They were destroying the library!

A high-pitched buzzing filled the room—Uncle Renald must have set off one of the security buttons in the wall panel. He appeared in the doorway wearing a plasticress breathing mask and holding a vial. No one even glanced at him—they kept throwing books.

He pulled the cork off the vial with a *pop!* and a gigantic cloud of blue smoke puffed out, trailed by a faint smell of licorice. The buzzing noise intensified but did not slow anyone down, except for two or three people who dropped the books they were holding and covered their ears. But as the blue smoke spread across the room, the entire crowd stopped in its tracks.

CHAPTER 15

AS THE LAST OF the blue smoke drifted out the open front door, the buzzing was replaced by the sounds of throat-clearing, coughing, and shuffling. There were murmurs, not shouts. People sounded confused, but not agitated.

Uncle Renald stepped to the front of the library, the mask now gone, and the crowd that had been throwing books off the shelves a minute before parted around him politely. "So sorry, folks," he said, holding a hand in front of him, palm up. "We seem to have had a small earthquake. Nothing to be alarmed about. As you can understand, for safety reasons we'll have to ask you all to head out, but thank you for coming on our tour. This way, please," and he pointed to the front door.

I expected an outburst at this blatant lie, but instead the crowd continued to mumble and nod as they filed back out the door and into the courtyard. On the way, the turtle-hat man tried to straighten a pile of books that had cascaded across a table, but Uncle Renald quickly told him his help wasn't necessary. The group calmly paraded past me.

Jane, Karl, and Florence hung back, looking wide-eyed at the mounds of books scattered across the room. I motioned to them and we followed everyone back to the front gate, which Uncle Renald managed to roughly shove back into place and lock as soon as the last person went through.

"Now," he said, turning back to us. "We've got some straightening up to do in the library after that little earthquake."

I assumed that he was trying to make this whole ruse seem like a joke, but Jane, Karl, and Florence simply nodded and headed back across the courtyard. I caught up to Jane and fell in step with her.

"What are you doing?" I asked.

She didn't slow her steps. "The curator told us to straighten up the library," she said.

"Because of an *earthquake*?" I asked, incredulous.

"You don't think there'll be another one, do you?" She sounded genuinely worried.

"There wasn't one in the first place," I said.

"What do you mean? There were books all over the place."

"Not from an earthquake, though, from all those people tossing them around."

She slowed then and looked at me as if I had been struck in the head by one of those books. "Are you feeling all right, Lydia?"

In fact, I was not. The courtyard was beginning to look distorted around me, the trees that normally lined its edges tilting at strange angles. Uncle Renald's face appeared in the middle of them, and I marched over to him.

"What did you do to them?" I demanded. I had never spoken to Uncle Renald this way before, but I was more scared of what had happened than I was of him.

"How interesting," he said. "It didn't seem to work on you. That was not entirely unexpected."

"What didn't work? What did you *do* to them?" I shouted. Jane, Karl, and Florence stopped and turned to face us, but Uncle Renald waved them on.

"I suggest you keep your voice down," Uncle Renald said, "before you upset one of the interns by spouting accusations about which you know nothing."

"Why did that blue smoke make Jane think there was an earthquake?" I tried again. "Why did that entire crowd of people believe you?"

"Didn't you notice the mess in the library?"

There wasn't an earthquake! my mind screamed, but I kept silent. I wasn't going to play along with whatever Uncle Renald thought he was doing. Clearly I was going to have to look elsewhere for answers. The words *They were made to forget* popped into my mind. Uncle Lem had said people had been made to forget about magic. Was there a connection between the blue smoke and magic?

I shook my head and followed the others into the library, where Uncle Renald handed out finger pads. The blue smoke had left some sort of dewy residue on my hands, and the pads didn't stick very well. I tamped them down as Uncle Renald was talking, but I couldn't focus on what he said. The library looked like a garden weeded with a bulldozer. Some of the shelves were completely empty, the books scattered across the floor and the tables and chairs. Some volumes hung off book cradles. One lay opened facedown in the middle of an otherwise empty table like a cat clinging to a raft during a flood. The bottom half of the book handler machine swung uselessly in the air.

How could those people have caused so much damage in so little time? How could I ever find my mother's book in this mess?

When I tuned in to Uncle Renald, he was instructing us on how to properly pick up the books from the floor. He didn't want them handled more than once, so we were to retrieve one book at a time and carry it to the closest bookcase.

"Don't you want them in order?" I asked. Uncle Lem had been extremely particular about having the books in alphabetical order by the author's last name. There was a spot designated for each letter, carved into the bookcases.

"No, put them anywhere," Uncle Renald said, wiggling his thumb as he checked his aer reader. "We have bigger concerns at the moment."

Karl, Jane, and Florence bent over and started picking up books. But I couldn't move. Put them anywhere? This was not how the library worked. I needed them in order so I could keep going through them, so I could keep track of where I was.

"Excuse me." Karl nudged his way past me to the nearby *A* bookshelf, delicately holding a copy of *The Westing Game* by Ellen Raskin.

"Put it there," I whispered to Karl, pointing to the *R* shelf. Maybe if I could get them close to some sort of order, I could rearrange them later when I was alone. Looking for my mother's book would now be monumentally more difficult, and my bookmark project seemed pointless.

Karl put the book where I told him to. It sat there like a lone loaf of bread in a basket.

Jane, holding a book, lifted her hand slightly, and I signaled which shelf to put it on. Behind her, Florence picked up a book with a *W* author—one my mother had described to me, about a young girl and her family moving across a prairie in a wagon. She glanced in my direction and then at Uncle Renald before dropping it on the closest shelf instead of the correct one, then turned to get another one. The book tilted and fell open, and I reached for it. As I lifted it, a circle embossed on one of the pages stood out, and my hand faltered, sliding against the page. The finger pad on my index finger slipped, and my bare skin, glossy with the blue residue, touched the circle.

Instantly, the air around me was blindingly cold, as if I'd been plunged into an icy bath. My feet were firmly planted on the museum floor, but instead of seeing the library and its shelves in front of me, there was a gigantic window, on the other side of which an unfamiliar landscape shimmered. The ground was a silent sea of waving grass, and the dazzling blue sky stretched overhead. Something flapped on the right, moving vigorously enough that it should have made a noise, but the air was strangely quiet. As I turned my head to look, the entire scene before me shifted and blurred like rain running down glass, then readjusted. The movement was coming from a wooden wagon parked near a creek, its canvas cover buffeted by a breeze I couldn't feel.

A sense of tranquility blanketed me, then suddenly the scene was gone and I was surrounded again by library shelves. Everyone was still sorting books—no one even paused to look at me. I turned the book I was holding over in my hands, but nothing seemed out of the ordinary. Fuzziness crept in, replacing the sense of peace.

Uncle Renald was wrong about the blue smoke not working on me. It had definitely done *something*.

CHAPTER 16

EXCUSING MYSELF, I WENT to the bathroom and scrubbed my hands before applying fresh finger pads. On my way back to the library, a blurry shape whirred down the hallway from the direction of Uncle Renald's room, but I was too discombobulated to follow it. I almost collided with Florence as she stuck her head out the library doorway.

"Did you see something go by?" she asked. I shook my head, not sure of anything.

We moved books methodically for hours. With the blue residue gone and my finger pads firmly on, no more strange landscapes appeared. Each book I carefully moved brought me one step closer to normal. But my finger still tingled where it had touched the circle. I wondered again what could have made the circles and why they were there—had my mother touched one too? Had she seen pictures moving inside a book? Karl's foot crunched a piece of glass from one of the table lamps that had tipped over in the melee.

There had been a piece of broken glass in the library the day my parents disappeared; I remembered Uncle Lem picking it up. But there had been no broken lamps that day, and I had been so caught up looking for my parents that I hadn't stopped to consider where the glass had come from. That perhaps it had been a clue.

I dropped to the floor in front of the bookcase Uncle Lem had been standing next to. Sure enough, there were several more shards of glass underneath the shelf, and a glint of silver. I pulled out a metal tool. I turned it over in my hand, squeezing the long gray handle that extended from the base.

"What is that?" Karl said, suddenly by my side.

"Aww, it looks like a little metal rabbit," Florence said, coming closer.

"It looks like some kind of stamp," Karl said. "For marking paper, maybe. Should that be in the Display Room?" He reached for it, but I snatched my hand away and put the tool in the pocket of my sweater.

I'd seen this tool before. The day my parents disappeared.

I lay flat on my stomach to see if anything else was under the shelf. Jane carried over a portable lamp and shined it into the dark space. Several more pieces of broken glass surrounded another object: the triangular vial that had been with the silver tool on my father's tray. It was on its side, rolled all the way to the back. I could reach it with the tips of my fingers, but when I pulled it out and stood up ready to examine it, Uncle Renald was standing there with his hand outstretched.

"I'll take that, thank you," he said. As I gave it to him, my ears burned at the smug look on his face. A liquid sloshed inside the vial, its iridescent color almost see-through, with a thin layer of bubbles skimming the surface—could this be what the mayor's office thought was a foreign object? But my father had bought the vial years before.

"Back to work, everyone," Uncle Renald said, holding the vial between his thumb and forefinger. "You're almost finished."

He must not have seen the tool, or he'd have taken that too. My instinct was to put my hand in my pocket to protect it, but I didn't want him to realize I had something else. So I worked diligently returning books, keeping both hands busy. How had the tool and the vial gotten under the bookshelf? The vial was on its side, which made me think it had landed there instead of being put there on purpose. It was a miracle it hadn't broken, although the glass shards implied that something else had, maybe another vial.

And could the metal tool make a stamp, as Karl thought? Had it made the circles in the books?

When the books were all placed on shelves, although they were still mostly out of order, Uncle Renald dismissed us. I stayed in the library after everyone headed out, then dashed to the dogwood fort with my hand over my pocket to keep the tool from bouncing up and down with each step. Inside the tree, I spun on the lamp and stooped down to open the alcove that held the typewriter. Pulling out the envelope with my name on it, I lined it up inside the round, mouthlike part of the tool and squeezed the handle. When I slid the envelope back out, there it was: an embossed circle with an open book inside.

My parents had been making the circles in the books.

I was afraid to touch it. When I finally did, nothing happened, so I ran my fingers over the rim of the circle again and again in a continuous loop, the way my mother had traced patterns on my back at night when I had trouble falling asleep.

Before heading out, I scoured the fort for anything else Uncle Lem might have hidden that could have been a foreign object. There was nothing other than the typewriter, its greenish gleam reassuring and hopeful. *Could* the typewriter have been the foreign object? From the front, it looked like all the other typewriters in the museum. Although when I shifted the typewriter to examine the back, it seemed to be connected to the tree trunk by a thin, flexible tube. I pushed my envelope back underneath the typewriter and pressed the rounded groove to hide it.

At the museum, I checked the backs of the typewriters in the Typewriter Room for comparison: none had tubes, but some of the models had similar-looking black cords. No, the typewriter in the fort was not a foreign object. With a gasp I remembered that the marzipan butterfly had been hidden in the fort too—and that Jane and I had eaten it. It had tasted especially delicious, but Jane and I had not felt the least bit strange after eating it. It couldn't have been a foreign object. Whatever Uncle Renald had used to make that blue smoke, however, was definitely something I'd never seen before. The man from the mayor's office suggested that the foreign object could be magical. Uncle Renald's smoke had caused the illusion of an earthquake and had made people forget what was happening. It had shown me the illusion in the book too. Had Uncle Renald found the foreign object—and used it? Worse, had the foreign object made my parents forget who or where they were?

I glanced in the Display Room on my way by, then stopped short. Something was wrong. Some of the items in the case nearest the door were out of place, jumbled as if they had been rearranged to fill a blank space. My eyes zeroed in on the spot where the Coconut Tyme matchbook should have been. It was gone.

I ran to find Uncle Renald. "Did you move the matchbook?" I asked. He was standing at the edge of the courtyard, knee-high in plants, parting a thick section of vegetation with his hands. He turned sharply when I spoke.

"I'm busy," he said.

"It's gone from the display case—did you take it out to examine it or clean it? Because if you—"

He cut me off. "If I need your help with curatorial duties, I'll ask for it." He shook himself out of the plants. "My hedgehog is missing. Have you seen it?"

"Not since the day you arrived. Has it woken up from hibernation already?"

He scowled at me instead of answering.

"Do you think your missing hedgehog might have something to do with the matchbook not being in its case?" I asked.

Uncle Renald twisted a corner of his vest between his fingers. "I left my door open," he said. "For a second. Before the earthquake."

"He'll turn up," I said. "He's bound to."

"He'd better," Uncle Renald said. "In the meantime, prepare dinner." I hesitated, wanting to show him the display case where the matchbook should have been, but he motioned for me to go.

On the way to the kitchen, I ran into Karl in the dining room.

"Everything okay?" he asked.

"No, it's not!" I didn't want to admit that the matchbox was missing. "Weren't you guarding the Display Room today?" I asked.

"Before the earthquake, yes," he said.

"The earthquake, right. Did you see anything suspicious? Let anyone in other than Uncle Renald and the first visitor?"

"Just you," he said, with a laugh. I didn't find that funny.

Earlier, he'd been arguing with Uncle Renald. He often seemed eager to help, and yet he seemed to be hiding something at the same time. I gave him a chance to come clean. "Is there something going on that I should know about?" I asked. "Between you and my uncle?"

His face froze in a half smile. "Curator Renald? No," he said, taking a step back.

There was something he wasn't telling me. I couldn't trust him. But I needed his help because of his aer reader.

Jane and Florence turned into the dining room, and Jane offered to help get dinner ready, but I told her Karl was already helping me and pulled him into the kitchen. I opened the pantry and programmed the first meal that was available—eggplant parmesan and vermicelli—realizing as I took the package out of the cupboard that we hadn't received our scheduled food delivery. Uncle Lem insisted that we keep our food supply considerably overstocked, so there was no danger we'd run out of food for a long time, but the deliveries usually came like clockwork. I'd have to investigate, but for now I had a more pressing matter. I turned to Karl.

"I need to check if Uncle Lem sent a message," I said. "Right away, please."

He glanced around to make sure Uncle Renald wasn't nearby, then pulled his aer reader from his pocket, tilting his palm toward me. He tapped with his thumb, but no projection appeared. He shook his hand slightly and the welcome icon began to glow when Uncle Renald's voice boomed.

"I'll take that," he said, and stretched his hand through the serving window. "And put it in my room for safekeeping." My limbs felt as heavy as stones. It seemed I was bound to get people in trouble, and now I had no way of accessing any messages. Karl's thumb hovered over his palm, and he pressed the dormant button before handing his aer reader to Uncle Renald.

"Finish preparing the meal, please," Uncle Renald said, checking under chairs and behind curtains as he moved out of the room.

I didn't know how to apologize to Karl. But he didn't seem to need me to. "Since when does the curator say *please*?" he said, reaching into the utensil drawer for table settings. But there was a worried shadow in his voice.

"I'll get it back," I said, burning my hand as I pulled the eggplant out of the programmer. "I promise."

Karl was quiet as we gathered around the table, but Jane and Florence were more talkative than usual, chatting about some of the titles they'd picked up in the library, and I joined in their discussion. Uncle Renald ate quickly, and instead of staying in his room as usual, he continued searching up and down the halls for his hedgehog. I thought about trying to dash to his room to get Karl's aer reader, but even if I made it in undetected, I'd be short on time. If I could get into Uncle Renald's room, I'd also want to look for any evidence of a foreign object and recover the museum's aer reader so I could finish checking the books—although they were so out of order at the moment it made me panicky.

"It'll all work out in the end," Florence said as I gathered dirty dishes.

"What?" I said, as the stack of plates wobbled.

"You look a little worried," she said. "But worrying doesn't help anything." She couldn't know what was going on in my head, but her smile looked so sincere that I couldn't help but smile back.

Karl challenged Jane to a game of mancala, and Florence insisted that she could find something more fun in the dormitory's game bin.

Jane invited me to play, but I told her I could use some time alone. While they headed across the courtyard, I cleaned the dishes. As the laser zapped away the last bit of melted mozzarella cheese from the plates, I imagined it melting away the past three months, undoing the days full of loss.

Too bad it couldn't melt Uncle Renald away. I needed him to be gone for a little while. The sooner the better.

I needed a diversion that would take him out of the building. Maybe he could go to town? He hated going there, though—he claimed the winding streets and staircases and the constant calling back and forth of neighbors gave him a headache. Maybe to the toolshed? That was on the farthest part of the museum's property. If Uncle Renald walked there and poked around for a bit, it should buy me enough time to go through his room.

Something scuttled over the top of my foot, and I yelped with surprise.

A spiky ball with ears and a striped purple collar peeked out from behind the cooling unit. Uncle Renald's missing hedgehog, out having an adventure.

"Are you hungry, little guy?" I asked. I opened a packet of dried vegetable cakes and held out several small pieces in my hand. The hedgehog nosed them from its dark corner but made no attempt to eat them. Then he moved forward and jumped into my hand, and as he did so, his whole body became visible: he was made of tiny pieces of metal bolted together. His legs were wheels. He was robotic.

He nuzzled the palm of my hand and nibbled on my finger.

I opened a nearby cabinet, threw several embroidered napkins into a bowl, and placed the hedgehog into it. He blinked up at me.

"You're going to help me," I told him, lifting the bowl. "Thank you."

Grabbing a lantern, I waited in my room with the hedgehog in my lap, patting his silver body. When Uncle Renald finally went back to his room after hunting up and down the hallways, I opened the top drawer of my bureau and took out my antique alarm clock with brass bells that rang loudly. I put the bowl with the hedgehog in its place, slipping off his collar as he curled up among my knee socks, then headed outside.

The toolshed was on a diagonal from the museum. The path that led the way was long and twisting, and the flickering shadows cast by the lantern beam kept startling me. "Why is the toolshed so far away?" I had asked Uncle Lem one day. "If you need a stepladder or a paint roller, you'd have to go all the way out there to get it."

Uncle Lem laughed. "Out of sight, out of mind!" he said.

There were other things in the toolshed, too, some of which were not tools: containers of potting soil, a toy rocking horse, and stacks of crates—the kind used before plasticress was standardized. A birdbath sat outside the toolshed, which my father had warned me to stay away from. "It's booby-trapped," he said. I couldn't tell if he was joking or not, but I had never seen any birds using it.

I set the alarm clock at its highest volume for the hour Uncle Renald would be taking his morning perambulation, and tucked it in the toolshed under an overturned wheelbarrow. Then I headed toward the front gate. My plan was to put the hedgehog's collar on the path nearby so Uncle Renald would find it on his walk and spend time looking for his pet. When he heard the alarm clock, he'd head to the toolshed to investigate, thus buying me the maximum amount of time to check his room. But as I neared the gate, footsteps crunched on the path. Someone else was out here.

I spun off my lantern and ducked into the trees.

At the gate were two shadows: a tall one outside the gate, a shorter one inside. Their whispers bounced back and forth in the darkness.

Their words were too quiet to discern, but one sound kept getting repeated: it sounded like *for* or *forn*. After a minute they both reached across the gate, as if shaking hands or exchanging something. Then the shadow outside the gate took off toward town, and the closer shadow turned and headed straight toward me.

I kept perfectly still. The sounds of the night were suddenly louder and slower. An owl hooted in drawn-out measures, and a critter scratched its way up the bark of a tree in slow motion. The smell of fresh dirt and broken leaves filled my nostrils. The shadow froze; more footsteps were approaching. Another shadow appeared, walking on careful feet to the gate, then crouched for a minute before turning and walking back toward the museum. The shadow nearer to me waited briefly, then followed.

I counted to one hundred slowly, then stepped back onto the path, leaving my lamp off. I dropped the collar on the ground near the gate, then hurried silently back to the museum. When I arrived in the courtyard, the door to the dormitory was open. A shaft of light fell on Karl and Florence as they went through the doorway. Which one of them had whispered to someone at the gate, and why? Maybe they were homesick and meeting with one of their parents. But it felt more secretive than that, especially if the *for* or *forn* I heard was actually *foreign*. Whatever they were up to, I didn't have a good feeling about it.

I waited until the door closed behind them, counted to one hundred again, then knocked.

"Come in!" said Jane, bright skeins of yarn strewn across her lap. Karl was dumping a bag of glass beads on top of a game board. Florence was by the window, her back to me.

"How's the game going?" I said, as I watched for a reaction from Karl and Florence. But Karl was intent on the beads, counting them as he slid them into two piles. Florence was fiddling with something on the windowsill. Had someone given her something at the gate?

"They haven't started," Jane said. "I'm knitting a scarf for my brother." She lifted up her needles, revealing a colorful rectangle.

"It's coming out great," I said. "He's going to love it." I called over to Florence. "Were you just outside?"

"Me?" she turned, holding a large, white blossom propped up in a jar of wet dirt. "Yes. I realized it was a perfect night to finally find a moonflower for my collection. They're nocturnal bloomers. I'm hoping it lasts long enough so I can photograph it when this internship ends and I get my aer reader back."

I had forgotten that Florence liked flowers. I'd never shown her the book with photographs of flowers and their symbols. Now

I had no idea where on the library shelves it was. "What were you doing?" I asked Karl.

He paused with his pointer finger resting on one of the beads. "I was looking for constellations," he said.

"Find any?"

"No," he said, sliding the bead to one of the piles. "Too many clouds."

"Why don't you play?" Jane asked, rearranging the yarn in her lap. "It's Nine Men's Morris."

One of them was lying about what they had been doing in the woods. I didn't know which one of them had met someone at the gate, but I was determined to find out.

"Okay," I said, and scooted next to Jane on the couch.

Florence scooped one pile of beads and shook them between her closed hands, blinking as they clacked together.

"It's a two-person game," Karl said, tapping the board. "Maybe we should do something else?"

I pointed to the mural on the wall that interns often added to during their stay. "How about painting?" I suggested. "There's plenty of blank space left. And we can play Truth or Lie while we paint."

"Sounds fun!" Florence said. She dumped the beads onto the table.

Karl didn't look so sure. "I'd rather not play a lying game," he said. "My life is an open book."

"What do you mean?" I said, half rising before I realized I was on my feet. Did he know about the book circle?

"It's an expression," he said, eyeing me. "What else would it mean?"

"Let's all do it," said Jane, putting aside her knitting. "Where are the brushes and the paint?"

I dug in the bin that held the art supplies and pulled out brushes and paint pots. Florence took one and started adding a vine to a border along the wall. Jane studied the cityscape and patterns that were already there, then dabbed bright orange spots in an area that looked like a park. Karl stood in front of one of the buildings I didn't recognize and painted a dark blue haze around the building, then green smears, then fish.

"Fish?" I said.

"It's underwater," he said. "I went there once. Everything was coated in slime, and fish were swimming in and out of windows."

"You went to one of the underwater ruins?" Florence asked, her paintbrush paused in midair.

Karl nodded. "With my family. We took a submersible."

"Wow!" Jane said. "Isn't that dangerous?"

"Not really," he said. "It was with a special tour."

"That can be our first question," I said. "What's the most amazing thing you've ever done? First round is a truth round, so you have to answer honestly."

Karl gestured to the painting.

Florence said, "For me it was a spelunking trip outside the city. I love caves! But I'd love to go underwater. How about you?" she asked me.

I thought for a minute. "I went to a waterfall with my parents and stood in the space behind the water." The sound of the cascading water was thunderous, and I was soaked from the mist.

"I did a nighttime scavenger hunt with my family," Jane said.

"You didn't just do it," I said. "You won it!"

Jane grinned and said, "That's true!" before adding yellow to the section she was painting.

Florence put down her paintbrush. "Okay, my turn! This is a lying round. What is your biggest fear?"

"Spiders," said Jane.

"Raindrops," I answered.

Karl said, "Flying kittens." His left eyelid twitched.

Jane said, "Third round you can lie or tell the truth?" I nodded. "Okay, how about this: What is your favorite thing about the museum?"

I said, "Curator Renald." Jane snorted.

Florence said, "Not having my aer reader."

Karl answered, "Guarding rooms all day instead of doing research."

"What would you research?" Jane asked.

Karl shrugged. "Anything. Even researching early styles of outhouses would be better than guard duty."

"Do you want to go next, Karl?" I asked. He shook his head. "All right, my turn." I cleared my throat. "Answer this truthfully: Did you go to the front gate tonight?" The atmosphere in the room shifted at the directness of my question.

"No," Jane said.

"I might have gone near it, looking for the moonflower," said Florence, pointing at the windowsill.

"Same here," Karl said. "I wasn't paying attention."

I cringed at their answers. "That was a bad question, sorry. Can I go again?" I didn't wait for anyone to say yes. "Have you ever come across a foreign object?"

Florence's eyebrows furrowed. "No," she said. Jane said no too.

Karl paused before answering. From our conversation when he sent a message to Uncle Lem, I knew that he was familiar with the term. Now I could find out if he knew more.

"No," he said, blinking hard.

I wasn't sure if he was lying or not. "Your turn to ask a question, Karl."

"I think I'm done for the night," he said. "Going to head to bed." He dipped his paintbrush into a pot of cleaning solution, then went to his room and closed the door.

"It is getting late," Jane said, yawning as we cleaned up the rest of the brushes and put them away.

I walked to the door, mulling over what little information I had gathered—but before I reached it, Florence said, "What is a foreign object? Do you have any at the museum?"

"No," I said. "I don't know much about them, to be honest."

"I wonder if that's what Karl was asking me about earlier. He was acting a little odd."

"What was he doing?"

"He asked if I thought any of the items in the Display Room might have strange origins or be from a different part of the world." She paused, as if wanting to know the answer herself.

"I don't think so," I said.

She laughed. "I don't know why he thought I'd know anything about them. He asked me if I knew where coconuts grew. How peculiar!"

"That is weird," I agreed. "Thanks for mentioning it."

"Anytime," she said.

Had Karl taken the Coconut Tyme matchbook?

I hadn't gotten the exact answers I wanted from the Truth or Lie game, but perhaps I had learned something important after all. And hopefully tomorrow I would learn even more.

CHAPTER 17

WHEN UNCLE RENALD STRUCK out for his regular morning walk around the grounds, I headed to his room with the hedgehog. I had initially thought Uncle Renald did his rounds for fresh air and exercise, but after what had happened yesterday, I now suspected there was another reason. He was worried about the museum.

Once he found the collar and the alarm and searched the toolshed, I figured I had fifteen minutes, but I wanted to get in and out of his room in ten, to be safe. The door was locked, as I expected, but I knew the code from Uncle Lem—he'd given it to me so I could wake him up if he ever slept through breakfast. The door opened silently, and I was facing the rows of buttons and knobs on the wall panel. I scanned the room—the bed neatly made, the night table with a glass of water, the bureau with drawers neatly closed and the hedgehog's empty cage on top. A desk was tucked into the corner under the window. All of the desk drawers and bureau drawers were locked. I slipped the hedgehog under the desk, and he curled up against the wall with a contented clacking noise. My hope was that Uncle Renald would find him and assume he'd returned on his own.

I crossed back over to the wall panel. None of the buttons were labeled, and I had only a vague idea what any of them did. I didn't want to set off any alarms, but if one of them opened the desk drawers, I could begin my searching.

One of the buttons on the panel was flatter than the others, worn smooth by touch, perhaps. Without hesitating I pushed it, hoping a desk drawer would click open. Instead, there was a soft whirring noise and a pop, and out of nowhere a door opened in the wall.

Uncle Renald had probably found the collar near the gate by now and would be heading toward the toolshed. I didn't have any time to lose. I went through the doorway—there was a wide stone staircase leading down, which opened into a gigantic underground cavern.

Metal tables filled the room, and shelves and cabinets and crates stood against the walls. One long, silver table dominated the middle of the room, covered with smooth steel boxes and cylinders, some cut with squarish slots at the top that emanated an iridescent light. Another table had a dozen monitor screens hovering above it, surrounded by consoles and projection panels, all powered down. Other tables were covered with racks crowded with bottles, tubes, and droppers, and were bookended by rows of microscopes and a round machine that resembled the centrifuge at my parents' workplace. There was an oversized basin with a giant turnip-shaped glass top, swirling with blue vapor similar to Uncle Renald's smoke. This was clearly a laboratory of some sort. Everything was neat and orderly except for one table covered with scraps of metal, bolts, tools, a mask like the one Uncle Renald had worn in the library during the "earthquake," and empty vials upside down in a drying frame. There was a plasticress box lined with tiny pillows, with a hedgehog-sized impression in the middle. It looked like I had been mistaken to think Uncle Renald was going to bed early every night.

Jogging around the room, I looked for the confiscated aer readers or anything that might qualify as a foreign object. Atop a rolling cart near a gray closet was a triangular bottle: my father's vial from under the bookshelf. When I picked it up, the liquid inside sloshed. I shook it close to my ear, then unsealed the cover a fraction. The sweet, new smell of the earth after a rainstorm escaped from the bottle and drifted upward, before I quickly closed the cover. Seconds later, the gray closet started emitting low beeps. The closet doors opened easily, and inside shelves filled with bins of aer readers stared back at me, some of them blinking as if they were alive.

At first glance, they all looked the same. It would be impossible to find Karl's, or the museum's.

Upon closer inspection, however, they were slightly different. The ones on the top shelf were oversized and had zigzag markings on the side—they weren't the models I was used to. The ones on the bottom shelf looked more familiar.

I grabbed one of the bottom aer readers and hooked it onto my thumb. The screen immediately appeared and the ID icon flashed a name that was vaguely familiar. It took a moment before I remembered that it was one of my mother's cousins who had passed away several years ago. I flicked the aer reader back into the bin, then reached for one closer to the top. The ID icon was green and rectangular, and I didn't recognize the user's name. I grabbed another from the bottom, this one from a bin that held three aer readers.

The name that came up was my mother's.

My hand shook so hard that the aer reader slid to the floor. I thought I had already missed my mother as much as I possibly could, but now, unexpectedly holding something that belonged to her, I was breaking down again, especially knowing that if I was holding my mother's aer reader, she wasn't. And therefore she couldn't activate it. I picked up the aer reader and shoved it into my pocket, then reached for the next one in the bin, bracing myself.

My father's.

Why didn't they have their aer readers with them? I could not let myself think about what it might mean that their aer readers were sitting unused in this basement. Instead, I shoved that one in my pocket too, as well as the third one in the bin. Then I grabbed a handful from another bin, hoping one might be Karl's, and stuffed those in too. I was running out of time, but I hadn't explored every corner of the room yet—there were more alcoves, more shelves, more cabinets. I would need to come back as soon as I could, but for now I had to get out before Uncle Renald had a chance to return. I ran back up the stone staircase and the wall zipped closed after me. I raced out of Uncle Renald's room and straight to my dogwood fort. It was still early in the morning—my breath was a white cloud in the cold air.

I pulled the aer readers from my pocket and put them on the floor in the middle of the fort. There were eight in all. I held my mother's and my father's in my palm for a minute, then slipped them on again one at a time. Maybe somehow I could activate them myself and stop the effects of the missing persons report. But there wasn't enough power to even try—their names flashed once before the aer readers shut off. It was the same for the other aer readers. Each brief glimpse showed that none belonged to Karl or the museum. The first five names that blinked on were ones I didn't recognize.

The last name I could read clearly, however, before it disappeared. It was mine.

CHAPTER
18

I DIDN'T KNOW I had an aer reader. I had assumed I wasn't assigned one because I was usually allowed to use the museum's. But I couldn't even get past the welcome screen on my own aer reader because it powered down so quickly. Taking it off and hooking it on again didn't restart it. There weren't any protocols that I knew of for addressing low power in the aer readers—normally they worked all the time. I put it into my pocket along with my parents' aer readers.

It was past time for breakfast, and I hurried back to the museum. Uncle Renald surely had returned already and was probably not in a good mood.

Everyone was gathered in the dining room eating breakfast. Everyone except Uncle Renald.

"There you are!" Jane said. "We were worried about you."

I looked at the clock—it was much later than I thought.

"Sorry," I mumbled. "Did you heat up food by yourselves?"

"The food programmer's pretty easy to figure out," Florence said.

"But that's my job," I said.

"We were hungry," she said, eating a bite of scrambled egg.

Karl straightened up and brought his dishes to the kitchen. When he returned, he asked, "Where's the curator?"

"He's not here?"

Karl shook his head. Jane said, "We haven't seen him."

Could he still be in the toolshed?

I crept down the hallway—his door was closed. I knocked softly, then louder, but there was no answer. Making sure no one was behind me, I tapped in the code, then pushed the door open—the room was empty.

The courtyard was empty, too, the wind blowing cold across the outdoor squares. Jane and Karl followed me outside. Florence trotted to catch up to me.

"Your sweater's really pretty," she said.

"Thanks," I said, looking down in confusion. Although I wore this sweater every day, she'd never commented on it before.

Her gaze stayed on my sweater pocket that held the embosser and now the three aer readers. The bulkiness made it slightly awkward.

"This place is starting to grow on me," she said. "What's your favorite item here? I noticed a gorgeous peacock fan in the Display Room."

"Yes, it's colorful," I said. She was talking about a folding paper fan that had the eye of a peacock feather painted at the end of each pleat. "I used to pretend it was a real peacock that came to life and roamed around the museum. I named her Turquoist."

Florence laughed and sounded almost wistful as she said, "It must have been nice to grow up here, so quiet and peaceful, with no one bugging you."

"I didn't grow up here," I said. "I lived in town with my parents before they disappeared."

"Oh," Florence said. "I'm sorry. I didn't realize." We kept walking on the path, the front gate in sight now. Jane and Karl were behind us but out of earshot. Maybe I could get more information out of her about last night, like if she had seen Karl at the gate. I opened my mouth to question her, but she beat me to it. "Where do you find things to put in the museum?" she asked.

She was awfully curious all of a sudden. But it was never too late to develop an interest in the museum. "We find some items at the Old and Useless Things Market," I said. "And sometimes people clean out their attics and storage units and donate things.

There's something you might like that Uncle Lem got not too long ago—a packet of dried flowers with an interesting label on it. The letters are swirly and hard to read."

Her eyes lit up. "Oooh, are they written in a different language?"

"I'm not sure," I said. "They might be."

"That sounds amazing. I'd love to see it. Oh, and what was that metal thing you found yesterday?" she added. "It seemed kind of unusual. Why would someone hide it under a bookshelf?"

"It's a library tool," I said. "I don't think it was intentionally hidden."

"Misplaced, sure," she said, sounding disappointed.

"Florence," I said, as we passed almost the exact spot where I had ducked off the path in the dark the previous evening, "when you were outside last night—"

"Gathering my moonflower," she interrupted.

"Right," I said. "Did you see anyone at the gate?"

"Like Karl, you mean?"

"Did you see Karl at the gate?"

"It was kind of dark," she said. "And I was digging up my flower. I didn't notice the gate." She drew in a deep breath. "Ahh," she said. "The air smells so fresh here." Then she said in a quiet voice, "You must miss your parents."

It was hard to keep up with her train of thought. "I do," I said, looking at the iron bars of the gate ahead of us.

"I miss mine too," she said, and when I looked up with a question in my eyes, she added quickly, "They're not missing or anything like that. They're just . . . not around much. I know it's not the same at all."

"Was that your mother who dropped you off?" I asked, remembering the lady in the business suit.

"No," Florence said. "She was one of my tutors. My mother couldn't make it."

"I'm sorry," I said.

She gave me a small smile, then took my hand and squeezed it gently before letting it drop again.

We passed the front gate but hadn't made it more than a few feet down the path to the toolshed when a voice called out to us from the road. For a second I was afraid it was another inspector from the mayor's office or an angry visitor demanding an aer reader—but it was a delivery boy from town. We backtracked to the gate.

"Food delivery," he said, stopping at the gate, out of breath. "Delivery boxes are on the fritz, so I'm delivering in person." He handed a thin plasticress box of meals through an opening in the gate rods.

"One box?" I said. "We usually get more than this. And it's never been late before."

"Be glad you're getting anything," the boy said. "Our aer reader system has gone bonkers. Everyone's orders are getting mixed up. The food factories aren't manufacturing on time either." He gave an agitated wave and took off in the direction he'd come from.

I tucked the box under my arm, and we continued toward the toolshed. As we approached, banging noises came from inside, and I nearly tripped over the stone birdbath that was now tipped over, bright orange water dripping from the bowl. Looking at the water the color of clementines, I remembered my father's warning and wondered if there was something more than rust in it.

I took a wide path around the birdbath, and the others followed me. The door to the shed was hanging open, and the noises now sounded like things falling over.

"How did you know he'd be here?" Karl asked. Instead of answering, I pushed my way into the dimly lit shed to see Uncle Renald tearing open the crates one by one and tossing them to the ground.

"He's got to be here somewhere," he muttered. "Where is he?"

The space was a disaster. Uncle Renald was shivering, and his shoes and socks were wet and orange, as if he had splashed through the birdbath liquid. As I crossed the threshold, his eyes were hot coals. "You!" he said, and I cringed. How could I be foolish enough to think he wouldn't figure out that I had sent him here? Who else knew about the toolshed, and had talked with him about his hedgehog?

But he didn't seem to be accusing me. He came closer, kicking aside buckets and sponges. "Where is he? Who took him?"

"I saw the hedgehog back at the museum," I said, hoping it might calm him down.

It didn't. "How did they find out?" he shouted.

Jane, Karl, and Florence hovered in the doorway. I hoped they couldn't see the crazed expression on Uncle Renald's face. What had happened to him?

"Find out what, Uncle Renald?"

"Don't play with me, child!" he shouted. "We have a thief among us!" He took a step toward me, stumbling like a toddler learning to walk. He tripped over a lumpy bag of grass seed and went sprawling to the ground, rakes and cans clattering around him. He ripped off his shoes and socks and threw them.

Karl rushed in and helped him up, both of them looking confused. "Let's bring him back to the museum," I said. "I'll make him some tea. He needs to be warmed up." Uncle Renald growled but allowed Karl to lead him away.

"Is he okay?" Jane asked.

"What was he talking about?" Florence said.

I didn't know how to answer either question.

Uncle Renald kept up a peculiar silence as we trekked back to the museum. When we reached the door to his room, he either wouldn't or couldn't lift up his arm to enter the code. I didn't want him to know I knew the code, so we led him into one of the spare rooms and got him to lie down on the bed. When I returned five minutes later with a cup of steaming tea, he hadn't moved an inch.

I took the blanket at the foot of the bed and spread it over his middle. The orangeness of his feet was fading, although his toes poked out from the end of the blanket like two pale carrots pushing their way out of dirt. As I was leaving, he finally spoke.

"Items are missing," he said. "People are looking." He blinked. "They'll be back."

I wasn't sure if "they" meant the items or the people. I pictured the angry crowd tearing down the books in the library. Uncle Renald's voice was low, and I strained to hear what he said next. "We can't keep it hidden forever."

"Keep *what* hidden?" I couldn't keep the exasperation out of my voice. "Did you find a foreign object?" I felt bad that he had suddenly gotten strangely sick, but nothing was making sense. While he was lying here incapacitated, I could go back to the underground laboratory and look for answers. I tried once more. "Uncle Renald," I said. "Did you find something magical?"

Uncle Renald hissed and lifted his foot, trying to roll on his side, then dropped his leg and started snoring. I could ask Jane to come in and sit next to him—to make sure he didn't get up and find me in the lab—but I didn't want to get her in more trouble. She'd already suffered enough for being my friend.

This time I didn't hesitate in Uncle Renald's room. The code, the button, the door in the wall—it was as if I had been born to follow this procedure. I ducked down the cool steps quickly, antic-ipation building between my ribs like a bird taking flight.

I tried to focus on what I hadn't already seen. I passed the crates and the cabinet with the aer readers and circled around the edge of the room, testing the other cabinets as I went. They were all locked. When I reached the far corner, where the room rounded off a little, the air felt slightly charged. A spigot of some sort stuck out of the wall.

As I leaned closer, the aer readers in my pocket started hum-ming quietly. I wasn't sure why they would work now when they had stopped working in the dogwood fort, but I took mine out and hooked it onto my thumb. It turned on immediately, scanned my thumbprint, and suddenly the words WELCOME, LYDIA were dancing on my palm.

Zero messages. I sent a quick message to Uncle Lem and checked the missing persons report countdown—it was still ticking away. I should have been trying to get into the cabinets, looking for a foreign object, trying to find Karl's aer reader, or trying to find the museum's aer reader, but I couldn't resist the whir of my parents' aer readers. I took mine off and took out my father's. It turned on and stayed on, and hope flared within me, but since my thumbprint was mine and not my father's, it couldn't access his reader. It hov-ered on the ID page.

When I tried my mother's, however, it scanned my thumbprint and made a dinging noise. LIMITED BIOMETRIC PERMISSION APPROVED appeared on the projection. It took me a second to realize that my mother must have added my thumbprint to her aer reader so I could access her info. It took me another second to realize what that might mean.

Had I reactivated my mother's aer reader? Would it cancel the missing persons report?

Would I be able to find out what had happened to my parents?

My palms started sweating, but I was afraid that if I moved my hand the aer reader would slide off or shut down. Instead, I stood as still as a tree trunk and moved my fingers as slowly as possible. I tried to click over to the mayor's page to check the missing persons status, but it wouldn't let me. I tried three more times until it dawned on me that I hadn't logged into my mother's account—her aer reader would show me only the single page that had appeared.

A page that didn't make any sense.

It looked like an excerpt from an old journal, with curly handwriting that looped and arched. As I tried to decipher the letters, the page blinked and the aer reader made a bleeping noise. Its power was fading.

I read as quickly as I could.

. . . has the power to cause great good, but in the wrong hands has caused great harm. That is why the Curators alone have been entrusted to care for it, to keep it safe for the world without the world knowing.

That was it. As the page blinked on and off, I tried again to click over to another page, to my mother's messages, but I didn't have access to anything else, and the aer reader gave a final faint beep and the screen disappeared. Frantically I slid the aer reader on and off, but nothing happened. Aer readers weren't supposed to shut off on their own.

Hidden in the far corner of the room was a dark cabinet—I pried the door open, but nothing was inside. I turned away to search somewhere else, but an unfamiliar sensation gripped me, and I whipped around to look again. There *was* something in the cabinet—a thin, brown volume.

As I reached for it, a shuffling noise sounded from above, like feet walking heavily across the floor. I grabbed the book, put it inside my sweater pocket, and snapped the cabinet door shut.

Before I had time to make it back to the stone staircase, the door swept open and Uncle Renald's bare feet came into view on the top of the stairs. Spinning, I scoured the room for a place to hide. The cabinets were too small to fit in, and the tables weren't low enough to provide any coverage. Uncle Renald's feet slapped against the stone with a slow, deliberate motion that still felt too fast.

There were twelve steps. By the time he reached the eighth, he'd be able to see into the room, and by the time he reached the bottom, he'd be able to scan the length of the room. I had less than thirty seconds until he spotted me. I turned toward the rounded corner of the wall near the spigot, trying to edge as close as possible to its darkness. A small carving protruded slightly from the stone—an open book in a circle. As Uncle Renald's feet came down another step, I jammed my thumb against the circle. A door soundlessly appeared in the stone, and with it, the scent of fresh water. I ran through without looking back, and the door slid shut behind me.

CHAPTER 19

I WAS IN A CARVED stone passageway with a dirt floor. It was dim, but not dark: a softly pulsing blue glow radiated from a recess in the corner. Over the noise of my heartbeat, I listened for the sounds of Uncle Renald on the other side of the wall. Instead, a murmur, like a tiny babbling brook, echoed in the cool air.

The walls and floor were smooth and clean, and there was plenty of room to move around. Stretching out my arms, I could almost touch both walls at once, and the ceiling was at least twice my height. I walked over to the source of the light, and the murmur turned into a gentle humming. In the recess, a stone tube, connected to the wall where the spigot came out in the laboratory, led to a round structure built of gray rocks that formed the shape of a well. Blue water shimmered up at me from far below, like a liquid night sky projecting its starlight upward.

It was water, but it was more than water: it was water and light together. Even with the well nearly empty, it gave off light strong enough to read by. The water was welcoming, its vibrations sending out waves of solace. The air smelled unexpectedly delightful for being underground, a mix of apple blossoms, freshly baked gingersnaps, and blankets warmed by the sun.

As I leaned over the well, the aer readers in my pocket started beeping, as they had when I was near the spigot on the other side of the wall. This water seemed to give the aer readers bursts of power. I quickly pulled out my mother's, but it still showed me just that one curious page. Why had my mother given me access only to that snippet? I pulled my aer reader out and checked the missing persons status—no change. Activating my mother's aer reader with my own thumbprint hadn't stopped the countdown. I put the aer readers back in my pocket with a sigh and examined a metal rack that hung on the wall above the well. It was circular, and held vials labeled with glacene etchings: TAN 118, WILDER 24, YOUNG 231, and dozens more. Each was filled with a clear liquid and dangled from the rack like the bells of a lily of the valley plant. Even higher above the vials, just below the ceiling, the blue water-light flowed in a long, vivid line that stretched the length of the tunnel and extended as far as I could see. I couldn't figure out how it stayed in the wall without running down the sides—it must have been surrounded by a clear tube, but it was too high for me to tell for sure.

Did my parents know about this place? The book circle that let me in here matched the book circle in the books—books that all had something to do with water. Was that more than a coincidence?

A loud *thump* sounded from the other side of the wall. I wasn't sure if Uncle Renald had seen me slip out, or if he even knew about this passageway, but I couldn't run the risk that he'd catch me, especially with aer readers and a stolen book. As far as I could tell, I was standing under the Mechanical Devices Room, but the only way out was either back into the laboratory or farther down the tunnel.

I sped down the dirt path away from the laboratory door, the way lit by the tube of water-light that continued overhead. After several minutes I slowed my pace. I couldn't be under the museum anymore, but there was no change at all in the corridor: it was one long, straight line. After a few more minutes, the ground started to incline up a bit, and, finally, there was a fork in the path. The water-light continued overhead, but an extra line spiked to the left along the fork. I followed the left path for several minutes until it ended against a dirt wall with a ladder, the water-light curving up. There was another book circle, a piece of glass smoothed into the dirt. When I pushed my thumb against it, a door slid open in the ceiling, revealing a sky so blue it hurt my eyes. I turned my head away and, as I did, a drop of something wet and hot hit my cheek, near the corner of my mouth. The pain was instant, and I slammed my thumb on the circle to close the door. I wiped my cheek, and a spot of orange—the same color as the liquid in the birdbath— came away on my fingers. They began to throb.

As I moved back the way I had come down the tunnel, the throbbing changed into a tingling feeling. When I reached the fork, I took the other path, and by the time I reached the end— another dirt wall with a ladder—my mouth and two of the fingers on my left hand were numb. The strip of water-light disappeared into the wall, near another book circle. I pressed the circle and ducked back as a door opened above me. I climbed up one-handed and peeked out—directly into my dogwood fort, by the alcove with the typewriter.

As I stepped in, the door disappeared behind me, and I turned to inspect the space where it had been. There was no way to tell that a door had been there, but for the first time I noticed an almost invisible book circle carved into a knot in the tree.

I sat against the curved wall to get my bearings, and the book in my pocket jabbed into my side. Pins and needles pulsed in my hand as the feeling came back, and I pulled the volume out. Its cover was soft and worn, but completely blank. Or so it seemed. As I tilted the cover, faint letters appeared like water trickling down a hill. The script was long and narrow, and the first letter, a *B*, extended from the top of the cover to almost the middle of the page. I tilted the book again to read the full title: *Book of Essence*. Essence, like the note on the typewriter. *When time is of the Essence.*

The same mesmerizing sensation from the laboratory gripped me again, and I opened the book. The first page was cream-colored and aged, but instead of being brittle or delicate, it was smooth and flexible. It was blank, at first. Then a dot appeared on the page, and with it, something flooded through me, an impression of beginnings, of hope. The dot stretched into a line and the hope spread, reaching out. It wasn't letters that were forming, but a picture. Each stroke evoked an emotion that increased the feeling that this was the magic Uncle Lem had tried to explain to me the day of the market: the comfort of sharing a meal after a long journey, the camaraderie of many voices singing the same song, the joy of inventing something useful to ease a burden.

But as the strokes continued, the ink changed and the feelings grew darker. Jealousy, greed, and anger. Then fear and fighting. Devastation. I could feel a sense of furtiveness, a great need to hide, to keep something secret. Not until the strokes had almost filled the page did it become clear what image was being formed: the museum. As the final tile was drawn on the roof, a burst of blue colored the page, and a sense of peace floated down. After a second, the blueness receded, leaving only a smudge of blue under the museum. The glowing water in the well.

Maybe I should have been scared: this book had a secret in it. Magic. But it was a magic that belonged—the museum was protecting it. This was not a foreign object.

I was about to turn the page to see what else this book held when the door to the dogwood fort was yanked open and light poured in around the silhouette of Uncle Renald, who blocked the doorway. As I scrambled to my feet, he reached in and grabbed the book from my hands. The image of the museum disappeared instantly.

"You are the thief!" he snarled, slamming the book shut. "My own niece, stealing from under my nose."

"No," I said. How could I explain that the book had called to me? That its story somehow belonged to me?

"Then where did you get this?" he demanded. I didn't answer. I couldn't speak.

He grunted. "Back to the museum," he said, moving slightly aside. "Now."

As I tried to move past him, I brushed into his arm holding the book, and it fell to the ground, splayed open to another blank page. I scooped it up, and a photograph appeared: my mother, Uncle Lem, and Uncle Renald as children, splashing in a fountain in the museum courtyard. I gasped. Hadn't Florence asked about a fountain in the courtyard? How could she have possibly known there had been one once, when even I didn't know?

Uncle Renald snatched the book. The photograph disappeared as he touched it. He turned it over and then over again.

"What did you see?" he asked, a thin edge to his voice.

Why didn't the book work for him? "The book is empty," I said, not exactly lying, because it *was* blank again.

"What else are you hiding in here?" he demanded, forcing his way into the fort.

I willed him not to see the compartment that hid the type-writer, willed a thousand invisible shields to screen it.

His eyes scanned over the hidden space and fixed on me. "You, of all people, stealing. You're not fit for the job, either, the one Lem stole from me. *I'm* older, you know. *I'm* meant to be the curator. Thieves, the lot of you." He pointed wildly in the direction of the museum. "Go!"

I went. We walked in silence until we reached the courtyard, and then Uncle Renald halted abruptly. We were standing where the fountain used to be. It didn't feel safe to ask. But I did anyway. "Uncle Renald, what happened to the fountain?"

His face turned hard as granite. "I suppose you think you're clever," he said. "The fountain incident was an honest mistake, a simple miscalculation. Everyone knew it. Lem. Your mother. But everyone acted like it was such a big deal. I was a kid, but no one would give me a second chance." He rammed the book under his arm. "So I've made my own second chances." He snorted. "The fountain."

I wasn't sure if he was talking nonsense or if the effects of the orange liquid had worn off. What did Uncle Renald do to the fountain? Uncle Lem's words from the kitchen came back to me: *No experimenting. Not after what happened last time.*

Uncle Renald brandished the thin volume at me. "You are never to touch this again. I don't care whether it's empty or not. I had higher hopes for you, Lydia. You've disappointed me greatly." He pulled a small circle from his pocket and held it up between his finger and thumb: the museum's aer reader. "You can say goodbye to this permanently, since you clearly do not have the museum's best interests at heart." His eyes sparked as he rolled the aer reader like a tiny wheel.

So this was my punishment. He didn't know I had my own aer reader now—although it wasn't working. The museum's probably wasn't either. But I hated that he had truncated my search for my parents. "Why do you dislike me so much, Uncle Renald?" I burst out. "It's not my fault you did something to the fountain. It's not my fault, or the interns', that you didn't get a second chance. We shouldn't be punished for things *you* did! So don't lecture *me* about having the museum's best interests at heart!"

He jammed the aer reader into his pocket, a storm on his face. "You speak out of ignorance. They were wrong about me. I'm the only one not afraid to really use the Essence, even if I have to wear a mask! I'll show them. Once they see my creation, they'll be sorry they let you pip-squeaks put your grubby hands all over the museum, when I could have been here all along, restoring the museum to glory."

"Did you say *use* the Essence?" It made sense. The Essence was the blue liquid, but he'd turned it into blue smoke to make the mob in the library forget. And I'd had some on my fingers when I saw the prairie scene in motion.

"Get out of my sight!" he roared. "Wait—first retrieve the items you stole from the Display Room."

"Stole? I didn't—" I started to say, but he held up a hand to interrupt.

"And don't even so much as think about prying into things you don't understand. The museum is not a playground. It will all come around," he said. "Wait and see." Then he turned so quickly that a vortex of fallen leaves churned behind him.

CHAPTER 20

MY MIND WAS A JUMBLE: the Essence, the underground tunnel, the book that drew a story of magic, more items missing from the Display Room. The photograph of my mother at the fountain.

Would I ever see my parents again? The knowledge that I had their aer readers and could not activate them made my body feel as heavy as lead. My only hope, other than them suddenly coming home, was finding traces of their thumbprints and activating their aer readers myself.

I wasn't supposed to leave the museum. I had promised my parents. And Uncle Lem could come back at any moment—I couldn't vanish on him. But I needed to go to my old house and find a print on a glove or a mirror or wherever I could find it. And maybe there would be a clue I had overlooked before—something that could be a foreign object, maybe. Or the plasticress box from my father's tray in the library. But first I had to find Jane and tell her. Since the day had gone so haywire, Uncle Renald hadn't assigned duties, and I didn't know where she might be.

On my way to check the dormitory, a message-sized delivery box careened into the courtyard and crashed onto the stone wall, skidding top over bottom before rolling off the far side. My stomach tumbled with it, as I dared to hope this was a message for me. From Uncle Lem. Or my parents.

I climbed over the wall and scooped up the box. When I pressed the OPEN button, nothing happened. The button for TRANSPARENCY didn't work, either, and I didn't risk pressing the button for SEND BACK.

The door to the dormitory opened and Jane came out. I raced over to her and held up the box.

"Is it yours?" she asked.

"I'm not sure," I said, unable to keep the optimism out of my voice. Delivery boxes usually floated directly to the person they were meant for instead of crashing into walls, so they weren't labeled. We wouldn't know who it was for until we opened it. "Can you help me?"

Jane took the box and we went into her room. She opened the suitcase at the foot of her bed and rummaged around an inside pocket, pulling out a screwdriver. Flipping the box over, she worked at it for a couple minutes. Nothing. Digging back into her suitcase, she pulled out a multi-tool set that included a mini-saw. I grinned. "You brought a saw?"

"All those hours helping Grandma Hastings are finally paying off," she said.

She sawed the end of the box open, then tipped out its contents. It was a video message, but the PLAY button was so dim I feared it wouldn't work. She handed it back to me, and I put it on my palm, angling it so we both could see, and then pressed PLAY.

The video was faint, but I could make out Jane's mother. Disappointment washed over me: it wasn't a message for me. Jane crossed her arms, gripping her elbows.

"The aer readers have almost completely stopped working," Jane's mother said. Her voice sounded a million miles away. "People can't access their accounts—their money, their food deliveries, their medicine. The transport cubes have stopped working. Some people have started evacuating to the city on foot. Dad is heading north to check on Grandma. George and I are still at home. Stay safe at the museum and wait—we'll come and get you if things don't improve."

I pictured the streets in mayhem, families with bedrolls hustling across the main square, mountains of unsent objects tumbling out of the transport cubes, men and women pounding their fists against the closed doors of the transport cubes for people.

It didn't fit with the neat, orderly place where I used to live with my parents.

The message turned off.

"I should go see them," she said, running her hand up and down her arm. "To make sure they're okay." She shoved the screwdriver and saw back into her suitcase.

The last time we'd had a conversation about leaving the museum, it had not ended well. This time was different. "I'll go with you," I said. I didn't want her to get in trouble with Uncle Renald, since he had forbidden the interns from leaving. But she was worried about her family, a feeling I knew all too well and didn't wish on anyone, especially my best friend. "We can bring them some meals in case they haven't gotten deliveries." Jane nodded. The museum wouldn't run out of food anytime soon, even if we didn't get any deliveries for a while. She grabbed her sweater and we headed to the kitchen.

"Do you mind if we stop in here first?" I asked, as we went past the Display Room. One look at the display cases confirmed what Uncle Renald had said: more items were missing. Everything was shifted again slightly, so it took me a minute to recognize what was gone: an advertisement for something called AstroSpace Peanut Butter that showed a boy eyeing a piece of bread spread with brown goo. And an orange card that said GET OUT OF JAIL FREE on it.

This was not good.

Who would have taken them? Karl? Did the mass of people during the "earthquake" have an opportunity to take them? None of them came into this room, as far as I knew, and I would have noticed if these items were missing earlier. None of the interns knew how to open the cases—I didn't even know the code—and there was no damage to the cases or the code pads. Maybe Uncle Renald had taken them so he could blame me or frame someone else? It wasn't impossible. I hoped that, deep down, part of Uncle Renald cared about the museum and its collection and he wouldn't have done something to hurt it, but I couldn't be sure.

"Is anything else missing?" Jane asked. I ran into the Mechanical Devices Room, then the Typewriter Room. Everything was as it should have been.

"Let's stick to the plan," I said, and we headed to the pantry.

Karl was sitting in one of the kitchen chairs, leaning back so far the chair touched the wall. He was tapping out a rhythm on his knee that I didn't recognize. "Hi," he said to both of us. The smell of meat loaf and green beans wafted from the food programmer. He had no trouble making himself at home.

"Do you know anything about items missing from the Display Room?" I asked.

"What? No," he said, letting his chair fall forward and drop into place. "What's missing?" He kept tapping his knee.

"An AstroSpace advertisement," I said. "And a rectangular orange card."

"I don't know anything about them," he said.

"How about a matchbook? The one you were asking Florence about."

"What are you talking about?"

I should have known he would deny everything. "Never mind," I said, turning toward the pantry.

"No, really, are those items missing? Do you need help finding them?" He was too earnest.

I didn't trust him.

He watched while Jane and I loaded our pockets with food packets. "Are you going on a picnic?" he asked.

"Something like that," I said. "We might try to do a little stargazing."

"It's light out," he said.

"Guess we won't see any constellations then," I said, and a look of surprise—or was it guilt?—crossed his face. He left the kitchen, and we slipped out the front gate. As we walked toward the town, I braced myself to see people running with luggage, to hear shouts and cries, but when the path curved behind the schoolhouse and emptied into the block adjacent to our street, it was empty and still. But extremely *messy*. Household items littered the curbs, and delivery boxes were abandoned on doorsteps. Windows were either tightly shuttered or left flung open, the brisk breeze sucking curtains in and out, in and out.

We went to Jane's house first—my house was next door, the shape of the porch and the curve of the roof so familiar it ached. If only when I pulled the key from its hiding spot in the window box and opened the door, I could walk back to how it used to be: my parents both inside, reading news projections or talking or making supper, even telling me to tidy up my room. But the house was empty, doors and windows locked up tight. Someone's abandoned pillowcase fluttered from a tree branch.

The door to Jane's house flung open, and before we could say hello, Jane's mother pulled us both into a bear hug.

"I told you to stay at the museum!" she said, releasing us, then hugging us again. She smelled of maple and cinnamon, and her embrace was sure and comforting, as if I'd spent all day outside in the cold and she was a crackling fire and a mug of hot chocolate. But her hug also made me wish that I could hug my own mother, and when her arms finally fell away from my shoulders, I had to blink away tears.

She didn't want to take the food at first, until I told her how much we had at the museum, and then she was happy to accept it. "Although I'm sure this will all be resolved soon," she said, putting the packets in her cupboard. "Once the technicians get the aer readers ticking again."

"What's wrong with them anyway?" Jane's brother came into the room. "Isn't it a bit odd that they've stopped working?"

"George!" Jane said. She hugged him and gave him the scarf she'd knitted, which he draped around his neck with a grin. It was the first time I'd heard anyone question how aer readers worked. No one ever asked how they were powered—it was as natural as the sun rising or birds flying. What I had observed about the Essence and its power over aer readers was not something I could share—the museum was keeping it secret for a reason.

"Wild times, don't you think?" he said. "You should have seen the streets, everyone rushing to get somewhere else. Who knows if the aer readers are even working where they're headed." He pulled back one of the curtains on the window. "Wonder if they're working up north."

"Your father will let us know when he gets back," Jane's mother said. "Which should be any day now." She turned to the cupboard and pulled out one of the meals she had put away. "Chicken and dumplings okay for everyone?"

She was including me in their family dinner. I'd eaten here dozens of times when I was younger, gobbling up delicious hot food and heading back out to play with Jane until darkness fell, but that was when I knew my parents would be tucking me in at night. The longing to have this again, for it to be okay to stay, was as raw as a hunger pang.

"I'm going to my house for a bit," I said, willing my stomach not to rumble. "I'll eat later." Jane was already reaching for plates to help set the table.

"Do you want me to come with you?" she asked.

"No, stay here," I said, stretching the sleeves of my sweater over my palms. "For as long as you need." While I hoped she would come back to the museum, if I were in her shoes, choosing between staying in my family's cozy home or going back to the museum and strange Uncle Renald, it would be an easy choice. Uncle Renald would be mad that an intern had left the program without permission, but with all that was happening, he had more to worry about.

The flowers that lined the walkway to my house were still alive. Jane's mother had probably been watering them. I took the key from its hiding spot and slid the door open, ducking in and shutting the door behind me. I tried not to think that if my parents didn't return and activate their aer readers, this could be one of my last trips here. I couldn't allow that to happen.

A cloud of dust floated in the air from the movement of the door. The air was stuffy, but otherwise everything was the same. I moved from room to room, saying a quiet hello to objects I had missed—the old-fashioned clock, the kitchen table, the quilt draped across the back of the rocker. I stood in the doorway of my room, but didn't go in. The door to my parents' room creaked when I eased it open. Although I had checked their room thoroughly for any hints of where they might have gone—even turning out the pockets in all their clothes—I couldn't help checking again.

Nothing stood out. I didn't expect it to be otherwise.

I took a pair of gloves from each of their closet drawers and folded them carefully in half. They hadn't been worn in so long that I doubted they had fingerprints inside, but I had to try. As I glanced over the items on top of their bureau, something caught my eye: a glass bottle, not a perfume bottle or a hand cream bottle, but one like those that hung above the well in the tunnel. It was clear, with letters carved into its side. They spelled *truth*.

The bottle was closed with a cork stopper. When I picked it up, liquid sloshed gently from side to side, like a tiny wave encased inside, trying to get out. The liquid looked similar to the one inside the triangular vial.

I put the bottle in my sweater pocket with the gloves, then headed back out the front door. Through their kitchen window, Jane and her mother and brother were bathed in a soft light, laughing and eating. I turned toward the museum. I would have given anything for what Jane had at that moment, but I comforted myself with the possibilities in my pocket.

CHAPTER 21

THE DOGWOOD TREE STOOD like a faithful sentinel, its branches rustling in the evening breeze. Inside the fort, I pressed the book circle and took the ladder down into the tunnel. The light was dimmer and the humming quieter, but the air was just as welcoming. After striding to the well, I took out my parents' gloves, turned them inside out carefully, and one at a time pulled the gloves onto my hand. Then I slowly slid each aer reader over the matching gloved thumb. The welcome pages flickered on, but nothing else. It didn't work.

I tried to hold my disappointment at bay. "Next step," I said to myself. "Keep going." There was nothing I could do right now about the aer readers. Or the countdown, the missing matchbook, the peanut butter advertisement, and the orange card, but I could continue my search for the book. I went back down the tunnel and out the fort and grabbed a quick meal from the kitchen before heading to the library. The books were all back on the bookcases but still shelved willy-nilly—even the ones we had managed to get on the right shelves weren't in alphabetical order. Books were standing next to books they had never been near before—it was like seeing the familiar ridge of a mountain range out the window every day, and then looking out and discovering that the line of peaks had entirely shifted.

Before I could resume my search, I needed to put the books in some semblance of order. Pulling on a set of plasticress finger pads, I started methodically moving the books back to their homes: I went to the *Z* shelf—starting backwards, as perhaps my mother had—and one by one plucked them. When I was dizzy from moving back and forth across the room, I sat down at one of the tables for a break. While I rested, Karl walked past the library doorway from the direction of the Display Room, but he didn't look in as he passed.

There was a mound of papers on the table, mostly bookmarks that had shaken loose from their books during the so-called earthquake and were dumped there while we were shelving. The bookmarks on top were ones I'd already seen. The grocery list with EGGS, BUTTER, MILK, FLOUR, TOOTHPASTE, BANANAS in red block letters. The one that was actually a bookmark, issued by the Podunk

Valley Public Library, with its hours written in the middle. As I was worrying about how to return all these bookmarks to their proper books, one I'd never seen before poked out of the pile. It was a photograph of the museum printed on gloss—a thin, shiny material used for pictures for a while after paper went out of style, before people stopped printing photos altogether. The museum seemed younger, fresher. There were flowerbeds everywhere, and a fountain in the courtyard spurting water. A young woman stood near the front door waving, and she looked like a picture of my grandmother that my mother showed me once on her aer reader.

The fountain. The one that Uncle Renald said cost him his place at the museum. The one Florence knew about that I didn't.

I thought of the lady from the mayor's office months ago, searching through the library, scanning items onto her aer reader, bringing the images back to the mayor's office to choose a logo— which had never appeared. Florence must have seen the picture at city hall when she was visiting her father. Was that what made her want to come to the museum—the fountain and the flowerbeds that weren't there anymore?

I needed to get back to work.

After I had moved another full shelf's worth of books, Jane came in.

"You came back!" I said.

"Of course I came back—why didn't you wait for me?" She watched me moving the books. "Why are you doing that by hand?"

She must not have realized that the book handler had been mangled in the "earthquake." Except when I took the cover off to show her, it wasn't broken. The piece that had been dangling before was now reattached, and it shone like it had been oiled and cleaned.

"Did you do this?" I asked her. "Did you fix it?"

She nodded, smiling. "Karl helped too."

"Karl?" I hesitated. "Why would he help?"

"I don't know—he likes books?"

"I think he's hiding something," I said, sliding a book onto the book handler.

Jane raised an eyebrow. "He seemed pretty willing to help fix it. It's Florence I'm not so sure about. Something about her seems familiar, but I can't place it."

"I trust her more than I trust Karl," I said.

"We don't know either of them very well."

"You're right," I said, and pressed the button to send the book back. "Which makes me extra grateful to have you here. And thank you for fixing the book handler. This will make a world of difference."

And it did. The handler zipped around the room, stopping in front of the book's spot, taking out the book that was wrongly there before placing the correct book back. The handler then zoomed the other book back to its correct spot and took out the book that was wrongly there, repeating this cycle over and over like a sped-up, bookish waltz until, finally, wondrously, every book was back in place.

Jane left to make herself some tea, and I sent for the next book in my search. I ripped off the pads and tossed them onto the table—I wouldn't need to touch the books anymore now that the book handler was working. I sent for book after book, trying feverishly to catch up. My aer reader wouldn't stay powered up, so I had no aid in scanning. As I had figured, many of the books with end-of-the-alphabet authors had double book circles embossed on one of their pages. Several of them had illustrations, and each time I saw one, my hopes lifted and then exploded like the seeds of a white dandelion head blown in the wind. None of them matched the illustration I had glimpsed in my mother's book.

A dull thread of pain was weaving across my temple when I found a book with a pale pink ribbon attached as a bookmark. The book itself was in poor condition, the cover bent and the title page torn down the middle, and many of the pages at the beginning were completely blank. The binding was broken enough that some of the pages were loosened from the spine. Usually a book in need of this much repair wouldn't be on the regular bookshelf but in the conservation section for Uncle Lem to fix. Had this happened during the "earthquake"?

The ribbon opened up to a page with a book circle. This circle had been pressed in three times instead of twice, as I'd seen in other books. On the page was a black-and-white drawing of a fancy outdoor picnic, with people gathered along a riverbank lined with trees. Birds and butterflies flitted by, and a spotted beetle crawled along a table laden with fruit and sandwiches and cakes. Everyone was facing the river, except for a dog sniffing a basket on the ground. A lady was petting the dog while looking at the water—her other hand was clenched, as if she were worried about something. Some people had their hands raised in a cheering motion, while others jostled the left corner of the page—people overflowed into the gutter between the pages.

There was so much detail in the drawing—the ladies' hats, the patterned dishes, the kids startling birds as they climbed tree branches. I couldn't stop looking at it. Something about it was vaguely familiar, but perhaps I'd been staring at it so long I'd gotten used to it, or maybe it reminded me of a picture I'd seen in another book.

But it had a book circle and an illustration of a crowd. This could be the book. Gingerly, I reached out to touch the book circle, half hoping and half terrified that I would suddenly be able to see the words as images even though I didn't have any of the blue Essence on my fingers. The book felt scratchy, but nothing else.

As I started reading the words on the page opposite the illustration, I sucked in my breath. Someone had marked this book. Not in the same way I'd seen words underlined in pencil or notes written in the margins of textbooks that were for the purposes of study, but thick lines boxing certain words, making them stand out like square boulders in a field of snow:

The emeraldine mossy banks of the riverbank sparkled in the morning dew, the shore spilling with spectators old and young gathered for the festivities. A silk banner rippled in the gossamer breeze, the embroidered "Upton Regatta # 212" displaying with a dazzling effect the excitement that was felt by all. One of the tables was filled with delicate sweets: chocolates and caramels; another with citrus and fresh berries; yet another with pastries and teacups of lemonade. *Brick & Mortar* was sure to win—even if she didn't, it was a beautiful day for a boat race. Through the dappled shadows cast by the waving oaks and elms, the sun was a vibrant yellow orb in the cerulean sky.

Together the marked words and characters were:

old # One : citrus & cerulean

It made no sense whatsoever. The two unfamiliar symbols—# and &—were nonsensical shapes like the ones on my typewriter. I had no idea what these words meant when put together, if anything. Perhaps a child had scribbled in this book long ago, practicing his rectangles. If this was the book my mother was holding, perhaps it was simply because she meant to repair it.

But the marked words *might* mean something. Maybe there was a way to figure out what the symbols stood for, at least. I had used the dictionary to look up definitions of words—maybe it had definitions for symbols too. Putting the tattered, marked-up book in a book cradle, I sent the book handler for the dictionary and flipped through. I didn't know what the symbols were called, if they even had names, so I couldn't search for them the way I did for words. But at the end of the dictionary were several sections: "Foreign Words and Phrases," "Biographical Names," "Geographic Names," and "Signs and Symbols."

There were hundreds of signs and symbols. My eyes raced down the page until I found:

& (ampersand): used to indicate "and"

It meant "and." How simple. I wondered why people stopped using it. I kept going until I found:

(octothorpe): used as a pound sign, number sign, hatch mark, hash mark, hashtag . . .

There was more to the explanation, including its many uses—such as a proofreader's mark for inserting a space—but none of it made much sense. How ironic to find an explanation for the symbol only to have the explanation so out of date it was useless.

I tried reading the first part of the words out loud. "Old-something-one. Old pound sign one. Old number sign one. Old hash mark one." They all sounded wrong, like a tulip topped not with petals but with metal, clanging parts. "Old insert space one."

I closed my eyes and repeated the phrases in my head. The only one that sounded vaguely possible was "old number sign one," but even that didn't sound right—until I shortened it to "old number one" and an image flashed in my mind of the Mechanical Devices Room. My father loved that room. He'd make up stories about the inkpots and the pencil sharpeners, how people of long ago went on quests to faraway lands to recover these artifacts. I always believed him at first, until his stories got too outlandish to be true. Then I'd add in details of my own until we were laughing so hard we couldn't talk.

Had he told me a story about "old number one"? Why hadn't I paid better attention?

I stared at the illustration in the book again, willing a memory to come back. Was this the right book? Did the message inside mean anything? My instinct told me yes on both counts. I couldn't risk this book getting tossed aside again or torn even more; I had to put it somewhere safer. Although it broke every library rule ingrained in me, I snatched up the finger pads and started to tuck the book into my sweater pocket, intending to hide it in the dogwood fort. My pocket was getting pretty full with the embosser and aer readers, and as my fingers bumped into the vial of truth mixture from my parents' bureau, Florence appeared in the doorway, her mouth forming into the shape of a question. Before she could ask me what I was doing, I yanked the book back out, but the vial came with it and fell in an impossibly slow arc, the etched *truth* spinning as the bottle turned in the air. It bounced off my leg and back up to where I could catch it. As I grabbed it in midair, the stopper popped out with the same noise Uncle Renald's had made when the stampede of people tore apart the library.

Truth. There were lots of questions I wanted answered. But there was one truth I wanted to know more than anything in the world: *What happened to my parents?* With this thought in my head, the blue liquid hit the air and turned into a blue vapor, and suddenly my mother was standing before me.

CHAPTER 22

"MOTHER!" I CRIED OUT. She didn't turn toward me. She didn't react at all. She couldn't hear me because she wasn't really there—she was a projection, an illusion.

She was looking past me, and I turned to see my father and Uncle Lem standing in the library doorway. "We have to go back," my mother was saying. Her voice sounded distant, as if she were speaking through a funnel. She was cupping her hands together, and opened them over a minuscule plasticress container—something small fell into it. Her words were faint. "I had no idea it landed on me. This is a breach of protocol."

My father took the box, said something about a new mixture, and ran out of the room.

Uncle Lem came closer and gripped the back of the chair by the book handler, the one I had been sitting in moments before. "I'll head to city hall right away. Explain it was an error."

My mother's head nodded like it was stuck on a loop. She sent the book handler for a book.

Their figures turned blurry, with wavy lines running across their middles. My eyes darted between watching my mother and trying to see which shelf the book handler went to. "Be careful," Uncle Lem said. " . . . dangerous . . ." and the projection dissolved into thin air, the book handler only halfway across the room.

They had been taken from me again.

A massive shiver shook me, an earthquake inside my body. The truth vial had shown me the truth in a way I did not expect. Two things were now clear: my parents had gone to a specific place—and Uncle Lem knew where.

"Are you okay?" Florence's voice broke through the fog. "Your face looks peculiar."

I blinked, and Florence came back into focus. "Did you," I whispered, "see any of that?"

"Any of what?"

"Nothing," I said, glad she hadn't seen it but also afraid I was losing my senses. It had been real, though. The liquid in the vial, whether it was Essence or a mixture—had shown me the truth of a moment right here in this room. It had power. And my parents must have known about it, since the vial was in their room—and my father had mentioned a mixture. Was it possible the mixture, or the Essence, had something to do with their disappearance?

Florence pointed at the book on the table. "Something to do with that?"

"No," I said, sliding my hands over it. "What brings you here?"

"I was hoping you could show me the dried flower label you mentioned earlier."

"Now?" I said. "It's getting late."

"If you're not busy," she said. I couldn't slip the book into my sweater with her standing there, so I sent it back to its shelf, her keen eyes boring into its battered spine.

Florence stood with her body angled away from me, but a square, brown object peeked from the hand she held behind her back. It was the *Book of Essence* that Uncle Renald had taken from me.

"Where did you get that?" I asked.

An unreadable look crossed her face for a second, then she pulled the book forward. "How could I forget!" she said. "I found it on the bench in the courtyard. I was bringing it to you to put back on the shelf." She held the book out to me, and I tucked it under my arm.

"You found this outside?" It didn't seem likely that Uncle Renald would have left it there after that lecture he gave me.

She nodded and wrinkled her nose.

"This one doesn't go in the library," I said, heading toward the door.

She followed. "I wasn't sure. All the pages are blank."

Before she could ask any more questions about it, I asked another one of my own. "Remember you mentioned a fountain in the courtyard? How did you know there had been one?"

She stepped ahead of me into the hall as I spun off the library's light. "I must have seen a picture on my aer reader—a brochure or something."

Inside the Display Room, there was a gaping hole where the packet of dried flowers should have been. This time the surrounding objects had not been rearranged to hide its disappearance.

"It's gone?" Florence asked. "Do you think Curator Renald is cleaning it?"

"No," I said.

"He didn't assign guarding today. Do you think someone crept in?"

"Karl," I said, the name grating against my teeth. "He went by this way earlier."

Florence winced. "I did mention the flowers to him. Just that you said they had an interesting label with a foreign script."

This was unacceptable. I had never heard of an intern behaving like this. "Let's go find him," I said.

He was sitting outside the dormitory bouncing a yellow ball against the stone wall even though night had fallen.

"Did you take the dried flowers?" Florence demanded.

He caught the ball, folding his thumb over it. "No," he said, looking from Florence to me. "Why would I?"

"You were in the Display Room not too long ago, weren't you?" I said. "Didn't you notice something was missing?"

"No," he said. "I didn't. I don't have it, and I don't appreciate being constantly accused of stealing."

"He could have hidden it somewhere," Florence whispered.

I couldn't allow objects to keep disappearing from the museum, especially when I had bigger things to worry about. Maybe I could catch Karl red-handed and end this once and for all. I beckoned for Florence to follow me, and as we walked away, Karl bounced his ball again in rhythm.

"I don't know how he's getting into the cases," I told Florence once we were back inside the museum hallway. "But I have a plan. Can you mention to Karl in a little bit that Uncle Renald replaced the missing flower packet with an item from the collections in storage? Tell him it's an instruction manual for"—I poked my head into the Mechanical Devices Room and pointed at a wooden machine that could write a duplicate of a letter as the original was made—"a replicating machine. Written entirely in a foreign language."

"There are collections in storage?" Florence asked.

"No," I said. "But Karl doesn't know that. I'll spend the night in the Display Room and catch him when he comes in."

"Catch who?" said Jane, coming down the hall.

"Karl," Florence said. "He's been stealing from the museum."

Jane turned to me with a look of doubt but said nothing.

"Time for everyone to hit the hay!" I said. "Hopefully by morning we'll have some answers."

In the corner of the Display Room, with my blanket and pillow, I curled up to wait. Before spinning off my travel lamp, I examined the *Book of Essence* again, wanting to rewatch the unfolding of the story of Essence and see the photograph of my mother, Uncle Lem, and Uncle Renald at the fountain. I also hoped it would reveal more information. But the pages remained stubbornly blank.

I thought about what the book had already shown me. That there was magic at the museum, the Essence. That the museum was built to protect it. I had seen some of what the Essence could do— make the aer readers work better when they were near it, change people's memories into thinking an earthquake had occurred. Show pictures from inside a book. And the truth mixture—which was surely tied to the Essence, or made of it—had shown me a snippet from the past. I was closer than I'd ever been to finding out where my parents had gone. "We have to go back," my mother had said. And she mentioned a breach of protocol—the same words the mayor's inspector had used when he was talking about the foreign object. My mother said that something had landed on her. Had that been the foreign object? Is that what caused the aer readers to slow down? And where was it now, or had my parents taken it with them? Had the foreign object—or even the Essence, if they were experimenting with it—hurt them in some way?

Footsteps tapped lightly on the hall floor. My whole body tensed, ready for the door to the Display Room to slowly open, but it didn't. The footsteps continued by, and I settled back into my corner.

It wasn't until I was already half asleep, lulled by the thought of catching the thief in my trap, that I realized I hadn't gone back to the library to retrieve the book with the message in it, my mother's book that I had been searching for this whole time.

CHAPTER 23

I AWOKE TO A strange metallic sound and was on my feet in an instant. Karl was fiddling with the lock on the display case.

"Stop right there!" I said.

He jumped back and put his hands up. "I was checking it!" he said. "To make sure it was secure. Florence mentioned a new item was put in, and I wanted to make sure it didn't get stolen."

I narrowed my eyes at him and looked into the case. The lock was still locked. Nothing was missing.

"Did you sleep in here?" Karl asked, but I didn't answer. With a gulp, I remembered the footsteps I had heard last night. I hid the

Book of Essence in my room, then raced to the library. Karl lingered in the hallway, watching me go by.

My mother's book was gone.

"Did you take my book?" I demanded, turning to Karl.

"For the last time, no!" he said. "I haven't taken anything! I'm *not* a thief."

"Let's check the dormitory," I said. "Make sure nothing new ended up in your trunk."

I stormed into the dormitory, tripping over a pair of muddy shoes by the door. Jane came rushing out of her room in her bathrobe. "Is everything okay?"

"A book from the library is missing," I said. "Karl was about to open his trunk and show us it's not in there."

Karl shook his head but opened his trunk for me to inspect. There was nothing but clothes and granola bars.

"Sorry," I said, although I wasn't convinced he was innocent.

"Maybe Florence knows something about it," Jane suggested. I remembered Florence's eyes following the book as the book handler returned it to its shelf. I knocked on her door and pushed it open. She was still sleeping, but her room was immaculate—my book was nowhere in sight, and the only thing out of place was a pair of socks on the floor. She stirred slightly.

"Florence, have you seen my book?" I asked. She sat up and blinked. Her glasses sat on her nightstand, and without them she looked like an entirely different person. Somehow familiar, as Jane had mentioned before.

Florence stretched as she got out of bed and reached immediately for her glasses. "No," she said, not asking which book I meant. "Why would I know anything about it?"

"You know someone is stealing from the museum," I said. "We can't rule anybody out."

"Why would I want something made of dead trees?" Florence asked. She stooped to throw her covers back on her bed in a bunch. "Especially if it meant something to you?"

"Dead trees," I muttered, offended. Maybe she didn't want the book. But maybe she knew someone who did. Why were there muddy shoes left at the door—had she sneaked outside last night? Her knowledge of the fountain—she had said her father "cleaned up messes" at city hall, but perhaps I was wrong to assume he was a sanitation worker. Maybe she meant metaphorical messes— maybe he was someone higher up, someone who could afford multiple tutors for his daughter, someone in the mayor's office. Was Florence stealing items—maybe things she thought could be a foreign object—and giving them to the mayor?

But she had given me back the *Book of Essence* last night, after she found it on a bench. Or claimed she had found it on a bench. And now that I thought about it, she had given it back only after I noticed that she had it.

"Did you go to the gate again last night?" I asked her.

"I was looking for more flowers," she said.

"Are you stealing items from the museum and giving them to someone at the gate?"

"I'm hurt that you think I would steal," Florence said, her eyes as round as an owl's, and for a second I had qualms about my accusation. When Uncle Lem told me to be welcoming to the interns, I doubt he meant accusing them of theft. I had now accused both Karl and Florence.

"Come on," Jane said, putting her arm over my shoulder and steering me out of Florence's room. "I'll help you double-check the library. We'll find it."

I wasn't so sure. I scanned the dormitory desperately for book-sized hiding places.

Jane led me away on heavy feet. I had finally found what I was sure was my mother's book, and I had lost it. Shaking Jane's arm loose from my shoulder, I ran to the front gate: there were footprints, but I could tell nothing from them, not even if they were new or had been there all week.

In the library the books were like colored stones of a mosaic, forming an elaborate picture but with a gaping hole where one piece was missing. It hit me: I was a thief of dead trees too. I had stolen the *Book of Essence* from the laboratory, with its blank pages that were not blank, and I had been planning to take the one with the pink ribbon and the coded message before someone had beaten me to it.

I was no better than whoever had stolen my book.

Jane and I searched, but it wasn't there.

Uncle Renald, who seemed to be back to his silent, sullen self, meandered in and sat down, watching us. He instructed Karl and Florence to dust the corners of the library. While they did, Florence kept up a constant, nervous chatter about nighttime flower blossoms and thorns and seeds, and about objects she had lost and then found again. I attempted, only somewhat successfully, to tune her out.

There was a loud *bang* at the front gate. Uncle Renald pushed back his chair so fast it toppled to the ground, its legs sticking up in the air. He dashed out of the room and into the courtyard, and we followed. A gray pillow of smoke billowed over the now-dismantled front gate, and a group of men dressed in black suits with red sashes marched toward us. Two were the inspectors who had visited the museum earlier, the one with the briefcase and the one Uncle Renald had turned away. The tall man in the middle was the mayor.

I wasn't the only one who recognized him.

"Daddy!" Florence called, as she ran up and threw her arms around him. He pried her arms off and she turned around with a smug look on her face. Jane watched her with a steely expression.

Florence *had* stolen my book. She had sneaked and lied. The part of me that hoped I had been wrong—that she had been interested in the flowers and the fountain—felt like a tree limb ripped off during a storm. She had lived with us and pretended to be one of us, but everything about Florence was fake. Even her glasses. Without them, and standing next to her father the mayor, I recognized her from aer reader newsreels.

The mayor patted her on the head, then walked straight up to Uncle Renald, so close he was almost stepping on the folds of the curator's long vest.

"Aren't you going to invite us in?" he said. "I believe it's time for another inspection."

Uncle Renald coughed as though he were choking, but remained where he was.

"Let's start in the library," the mayor said, and led his entourage into the museum, leaving Uncle Renald no choice but to trot after them. They stopped in the library, and Jane, Karl, and I filed into the doorway. The mayor crossed the room, glancing in disgust at the thousands upon thousands of rare books like they were common weeds.

"This museum is in a tight spot," he said. "Failing quality control inspections, refusing entry and basic courtesy to inspectors *and* visitors on numerous occasions—"

"Not precisely the circumstances," Uncle Renald said, but the mayor kept talking.

"—failing to file appropriate reports and statistics in a timely manner, all of which make me incredibly disposed to permanently cut off your funding and claim this property for something that will be useful and welcoming to all—my new initiative, a family-centered park." He looked around. If he expected nods and murmurs of approval, he was disappointed. We were silent.

"I hardly think—" began Uncle Renald, but the mayor cut him off.

"And I haven't even mentioned the worst offense yet, which by itself is worthy of shutting you down: harboring a foreign object and lying about it. I was informed months ago that the breach of protocol alert I received was simply a technological error, but that appears, unfortunately, not to have been the case, as the functionality of the aer readers has been on a continuous decline since that object first blipped onto the radar. Your running of this so-called institution has been called into considerable question, and I have been granted special dispensation over the museum to come here and dispose of the object. And then we will discuss the future of this place. So, kindly hand over the foreign object."

Uncle Renald stepped back, holding his hands up. "I don't know what you're talking about," he said, and the mayor laughed a hard laugh. He flicked on his aer reader and made several quick jabs at it before it turned off.

"I have accelerated the countdown activated by the missing persons report," he said. "Your time at the museum has been considerably shortened." A stone plunged to the bottom of my stomach.

"What countdown? What report?" Uncle Renald still didn't know what I had done.

The mayor said, "Perhaps your young ward can fill you in." Uncle Renald turned to me.

"I wanted to find my parents," I said, wringing my hands. "I didn't know they could take our house away, and the museum."

"Our family is charged with protecting this place," Uncle Renald said, his voice low but oscillating with anger. "You claimed I was the one who didn't have the museum's best interests at heart, and this is what you've been doing?"

"I've been trying to find a way to stop it!"

"If we lose the museum," Uncle Renald said, "the blame will be yours."

"What a touching family moment," the mayor said. "Please fetch the foreign object immediately, and we can put this unfortunate business behind us."

Florence walked up to me like a cat stalking a bird, and I stiffened—then suddenly she plunged her hand into my sweater pocket and pulled out the embosser. I swatted at her but not fast enough. "This might be it!" she called out and jumped to hand it to the mayor.

He turned it over a few times, then shook his head. "This isn't anything important," he said, and tossed it away. Heat spread from the top of my ears down to my earlobes, arcing in the same path the embosser took as it crashed to the floor.

I stepped through the doorway. "There is no foreign object here," I said, as loudly as I dared. I remembered my mother's voice fading in and out and using the mayor's same words, *breach of protocol*. "This is all a mistake."

The mayor barely flicked his eyes at me. "One last chance to turn it over, Mr. Curator," he said.

Uncle Renald stood as still as a stone pillar.

"I know something else it could be," Florence said cheerfully. "He keeps it in his room. I'll go get it." Whatever she thought was in Uncle Renald's room, she wouldn't be able to get in without the code. I glanced over at Uncle Renald. His hands were clenched tightly at his sides.

"Do that," the mayor said.

As Florence skipped out of the room, one of the mayor's men came forward with a plasticress bag. It was the briefcase man—his quality control inspection had been a complete farce from the beginning.

He dumped the contents of the bag onto the table. Out tumbled all the objects Florence had apparently considered suspicious enough to pass on to the mayor's office via the front gate: the Coconut Tyme matchbook, the peanut butter advertisement, the orange GET OUT OF JAIL FREE card, and the packet of dried flowers, as well as a vial, which I hadn't known was missing. It must have been the one Uncle Renald left in the library after he made the blue smoke. The damaged book with the pink ribbon bookmark fell out of the bag last, landing with a *thump* on the table. I edged as close to it as I could.

Florence marched triumphantly into the library, holding the hedgehog's cage. Uncle Renald let out a snarl and grabbed for it. "You have no right to that. How did you access my room?"

She swung the cage out of his reach, and one of the mayor's men stepped in front of Uncle Renald. "It wasn't hard," Florence said. "It's the same code as the locks on the display cases, which I learned pretty early on. Not exactly difficult to peek over your shoulder."

I hoped against hope that Florence hadn't discovered the laboratory under Uncle Renald's room. She seemed so pleased with her undercover work that she probably would have gloated if she had, so I breathed a little easier. Uncle Renald, however, didn't seem to be breathing at all. His eyes were glued to the cage as Florence plunked it down on the table next to the stolen items. The table shook as she did so, and the vial rolled to the end nearest me. I reached for it, but it rolled off, hit the floor, and cracked. A mist of blue smeared across my thumb and forefinger.

No one looked my way—they were all staring at the cage.

"Leave it alone, please, Mr. Mayor," said Uncle Renald. "This isn't what you're looking for."

"I'll be the judge of that," said the mayor, lifting the top off the cage. The hedgehog was curled into a spiky orb. The mayor reached in and picked him up. The hedgehog squirmed, his ears and the black tip of his snout quivering. He was so realistic he was almost alive.

The mayor rolled him around in his hand, and as he did the wheels popped into view and the mayor jerked his arm. The animal's row of steely spikes stood on end, jabbing sharply into the mayor's palm.

Yelping, the mayor dropped the hedgehog. He scuttled across the floor straight to Uncle Renald, who reached down to scoop him up. But one of the mayor's men got him first. The hedgehog blinked with eyes that were tiny marbles.

"This creature," the mayor said, rubbing his sore hand, "must be the foreign object. If we dispose of it, the aer readers' power will be restored." He turned to the man holding the hedgehog. "Take it outside and destroy it."

"No!" Uncle Renald cried. "This is years' worth of my work!" He moved to snatch the hedgehog, but one of the mayor's inspectors grabbed Uncle Renald's arms and pinned them behind his back. Horrified, I ran to the doorway. Jane was hovering beyond it, out of view of the others in the room. As the man approached, Karl stepped toward him, dragging his foot slightly. The man tripped and tumbled to the ground. The hedgehog flew through the air and into my hands.

A tingling sensation rushed through my fingertips where the blue substance had touched it minutes before. If I hadn't been holding the creature in my own two palms, I'm not sure I would have believed what happened next. The hedgehog's metal pieces softened into hairlike spines, and its wheels morphed into feet that kicked at the air. Jane gasped and Florence shrieked as the animal looked around with eyes that were wide and soft. The hedgehog was now a living creature.

CHAPTER 24

"WHAT MAGIC IS THIS?" the mayor roared. "Seize her!"

I turned my back to the mayor and his men and slipped the hedgehog to Jane. "Bring him to the dogwood fort," I whispered. She nodded and darted down the hall. Then I crouched, clutching my hands to my chest as if I still had the hedgehog, but the mayor's man closest to me grabbed my wrists and slapped on a pair of magnetized gloves. I could not move my hands, no matter how strongly I tried to pull them apart.

"Where is it?" the mayor yelled. I mimed searching on the floor, hoping they would think it had run under one of the bookcases. The mayor made a quick motion with his hand, and one of the men dropped to his knees to hunt, while two others grabbed Uncle Renald and Karl and bound their hands with magnetized gloves too. Florence stood against one of the bookshelves, her eyes jumping back and forth between her father and our handcuffs.

"You don't seem to understand the situation, Mr. Curator," the mayor said. "The aer readers have failed. There is widespread pandemonium. And now I find you're using magic at the museum? Magic, which has been banned for centuries?"

"Banned for some," he muttered.

"What did you say? Speak up!" said the mayor.

"It's not what you think," I said. Even though I didn't understand the museum's secret, it needed to be kept. "I don't know how to do magic."

Karl spoke up, "There is likely a scientific component to it. If you would unbind us, I'm sure we could figure it out."

The mayor ignored him. "This museum is a threat to our community," he said. "And we're going to take care of that. Start with giving me some answers. *Is* the hedgehog the foreign object?"

"No," Uncle Renald said. He glanced toward his room, perhaps calculating whether he could make a run for it and grab a round of blue forgetting smoke, if he had any left. One of the mayor's men shifted position and blocked the doorway.

"Then what is?"

Uncle Renald shook his head. "There isn't one here."

The mayor plucked a book off a shelf.

"*Little House on the Prairie*," he read. "Sounds disgustingly cute." He reached for the Coconut Tyme matchbook sprawled on the table and opened it, revealing two matches. "Where is the foreign object, Mr. Curator? Answer quickly. Time is of the essence here."

His sentence rang in my head. It was eerily similar to the message in the fort. *When time is of the Essence, type what you've always wanted to type.* Did it mean a situation like this? Was time of the essence now?

I didn't have time to decide, because suddenly there was a crinkly sound and an unfamiliar acrid smell. The mayor had lit one of the matches. He was holding it to the bottom corner of the book's open pages, and the flames were licking up the edges of the paper, eating it greedily in curling yellow and orange gulps.

That someone would actually burn a book—that I was watching it disappear—felt like I was caught in the lurch of the earth stopping on its axis. I had seen inside that book, that prairie with the beautiful blue sky all around, the wind blowing the canvas on the wagon—how could anyone let that burn? I steadied my feet and rushed at the mayor, swinging my immobilized hands in an attempt to knock the book away from him. He simply stepped aside and held the book higher. One of his men grabbed my shoulders and crooked his arm across my torso. As more pages caught on fire, another of the mayor's men opened a window to let the smoke out. The mayor dropped the book to the ground, and it shriveled into a lump of wilted gray and black. I screamed.

"Remove her from this room," the mayor commanded.

Florence stepped forward. "There's a toolshed," she said. "You could keep her there."

"Perfect," said the mayor. "At least you managed to learn *something* useful while you were here." The mayor was still speaking as the man holding me prisoner pushed me through the doorway. "I can do this all day, Mr. Curator," he said. "There are plenty of books here." There was a scraping sound, like chairs being shoved, and I pictured Uncle Renald charging at the mayor to stop him. Instead, when footsteps clomped behind me and I twisted around, Karl was being marched out. He knocked into the table, sending the hedgehog's cage and the book with the pink ribbon to the ground with a crash.

"Last chance," the mayor said. "It would be a shame for the museum to *accidentally* burn down before we locate the foreign object, especially since the collection is composed of such excellent fodder for fire." He ran his hand along a bookshelf, dumping its books into a pile under the window, then lit the second match.

"Stop," Uncle Renald said, his voice thick and broken. "The hedgehog is the foreign object. Please, leave the museum alone." His voice faded as I was led down the hall. But the mayor's voice boomed out.

"Better help us find it then, Mr. Curator. Although I have a feeling that even after we do, there will be nothing left of the poor museum but a wide-open space."

I kicked and struggled the entire way to the toolshed, but my captor's hold did not loosen. Trying to pull my hands apart did nothing—they were practically welded together by the strong magnets. The men locked Karl and me in the toolshed, and I waited for my eyes to adjust to the darkness, each pounding of my heart pushing the dimness a beat away. A thin spine of light showed under the bolted double door. Pinholes of brightness shone in from circles in the wood made by woodpeckers or carpenter bees. The contents of the shed were dark lumps, some with parts sticking out.

"I need to escape!" I said. The smell of the burned book was stuck in my throat.

Karl answered from farther away than I expected. "We need a plan," he said.

I steadied my pulse, listening to the sounds of the mayor's men outside and trying to figure out if they were standing guard or if they had walked away. Someone coughed from the front outside corner of the shed. One of them, at least, was still out there.

"I know a trick to get the gloves off," Karl said. "Curator Lem taught me. Instead of trying to pull—"

"You know Uncle Lem?" I interrupted, a strange mix of relief and uncertainty gathering in my insides. Uncle Lem had taught me a trick too. He had a set of super strong toy magnets shaped like triangles and squares that I loved to build with—but when I wanted to take the magnets apart to build something else, pulling and yanking did not loosen them. Uncle Lem showed me how to push the magnets toward each other and then slide them away, instead of trying to pull them apart. The gloves worked the same way: pulling my hands apart, which is what anyone would do while struggling to get free, required too much force to overcome the magnets. To get free, I had to do the opposite of what it seemed I should do.

"I've known Curator Lem for a while," Karl admitted. "My father is on the Historical Architecture Oversight Committee with him and always dragged me to meetings. Curator Lem noticed that I was bored and starting bringing along games for me. One night he brought gloves like these ones"—a shuffling sound like he was lifting his hands—"and let me play with them. When he found out my final internship was overbooked and I needed to do another one before I could take the qualifying exam, he invited me to come here. And then, right before we came, he asked me if I wouldn't mind looking out for you, in case you needed help with anything. But he asked me to do it without letting you know."

He sounded guilty—and no wonder, because he should have told me sooner.

"I'm afraid I haven't helped much. Although I did try to follow Florence one night when she went out in the dark, but I wasn't quick enough. Anyway, the trick to the gloves is—"

"Slide them away," I said. I'd been trying the whole time he was talking, but the magnets were extremely strong. Working in the low light, focusing on feel and intuition, kept me from panicking about the museum. Finally, the gloves started to move.

Karl was still talking. "Curator Lem gave me an aer reader to keep safe for you because he was afraid Curator Renald might not give you a set of instructions he was supposed to. But he said the information on it had to be held by a neutral party until the end of the month. He was very specific about the date. That's why I had two aer readers. Although when I handed one to my mom on our first day here," he gulped, "I gave her the wrong one. The second one should have recognized your thumbprint even if it was too early to open the data." I hoped he was working on his magnets while he was talking. "I tried to get permission to go home and get it after I realized the biometrics didn't work on you, but Curator Renald refused."

"That's why you were arguing with him," I said. With a final effort, the gloves separated. I put one hand behind my back to keep it from reattaching to the other glove, which I held between my knees while I wrenched my other hand free. Rubbing my sore wrists, I said, "You loose?"

"Almost," he said, and while he worked I peeked out one of the holes in the wood. One of the mayor's men had stayed to keep guard, and he stood halfway between the shed door and the fallen birdbath. Beyond him, back toward the courtyard, thin smoke trailed upward. Even though it was not close, it was choking me. The mayor was burning more books, Uncle Renald was being held hostage, and I didn't know if Jane was okay.

As I stepped away from the wooden peephole, a memory hit me. I was five years old, peering out from behind the wooden legs of the printing press in the Mechanical Devices Room, watching for my father. We were playing a spying game we had made up after my father had explained the history of the printing press to me, that it had been used by a printer during a war to print a newspaper called the *Spy*, a printer who had nicknamed his printing press "Old Number One" because it was his first press and it was tried and true. "Old # One" was the printing press! And it was in imminent danger of being turned into ash.

I wanted to break out of the shed and run straight to the museum. But I had already proven myself ineffective against the mayor. Even if I had that aer reader from Uncle Lem, it wouldn't work. I had to use the tools at hand.

When time is of the Essence, type what you've always wanted to type.

I needed to head away from the flames I so desperately wanted to stop. I needed to get to my dogwood fort without being seen.

The mayor's man was pacing near the tipped-over birdbath. Behind me, Karl clambered over a pile in the dim light, and something metal clanged to the ground. The mayor's man turned around and squinted at the shed.

"Make more noise," I said. "I need a diversion."

"What's your plan?" Karl asked.

"I'm going to make a run for it, and I need you to cover for me," I said, my eye still on the mayor's man. He had turned back around, facing away from us.

"What about me?"

"There's something I need to do," I told him. The smell of smoke was getting stronger. "We don't have much time!"

Karl picked up the metal object—it was a garden rake—and started banging it against a barrel. "Help!" he yelled. The mayor's man rushed to the front door but didn't open it.

"What's going on?" he called.

"I think the girl's hurt," Karl said. He kept banging on the barrel. I stood next to the door, willing the mayor's man to slide it open. He did, slowly, standing on the threshold and peering in.

"She's back in the far corner," Karl said, and I silently thanked him as the man stepped past my dark hiding place and I slipped out the door. I ran for the birdbath. I had only seconds before he would realize he was being tricked and come after me, but from my trip through the underground tunnel, the flash of blue sky and the drip of orange, I was confident I could find what had to be there. And it was there, embossed in cement near the birdbath's base: an open book in a circle.

When I pressed on the circle, the door slid open, and I scrambled down the ladder embedded in the dirt wall. The door closed above me before my feet reached the floor of the tunnel. I didn't stop moving even when my left arm started aching—some of the orange liquid must have touched me on my way past the birdbath. The water-light lining the walls was faint, flickering in spots. I bolted down the earthen path, bursting into the dogwood fort out of breath, Uncle Lem's refrain echoing in my head.

Jane looked up in surprise, and the hedgehog chittered. I hugged them both quickly. "I have to do something," I said, and she nodded. "You might want to wait outside. I'm not exactly sure what's going to happen."

"Do you need help?" she asked.

So many people willing to help me. But I needed to do this on my own, so I shook my head and waited until she was outside the tree.

I opened the hidden compartment. My typewriter was waiting, its green metal shining.

The piece of paper faced me like an endless horizon.

I hovered my fingers over the keys. My left elbow felt numb. My hands trembled so much I was afraid that I wouldn't be able to type.

Calm down, I told myself, and tried not to think of all the books in the library going up in flames. All those pages with words turning into nothingness. My chance at finding my parents— evaporating into ash and dust.

I took a deep, ragged breath. *Type what you've always wanted to type.*

Something would happen when I typed, something even more than the magic of letters appearing on a page. The museum would be different. It wouldn't be the same place where I had lived for the past few months while waiting for my parents. It wouldn't be the same place I came with my parents to visit Uncle Lem, when I spent hours in the library, soaking in books. It wouldn't be my bookmark collection and the neatly alphabetized books, the cascade of typewriters on display.

But already, it wasn't that. Perhaps it could never be that again.

I swallowed a lump in my throat. I might be pressing a self-destruct button. The museum might be destroyed—maybe by blue smoke, and none of us would ever remember the museum ever again.

But even that might not be worse than what was happening to it now.

I put my finger on the shift key for a capital letter, the way Uncle Lem had explained to me one rainy afternoon in the Typewriter Room. The cool, silver circles felt grooved for my fingertips alone. I pushed hard on the letter *T*. The metallic clang of the letter wheel hitting the paper reverberated throughout the tree fort.

And, just like that, there was a letter on the page. A new shape. I had put a star in the sky and had the power to add thousands upon thousands more.

I'd expected the ink to be black, like all the samples in the museum, but it was a vibrant blue. I tapped the next key cautiously, not wanting to make a mistake but also trying to catch the moment as the letter appeared on the paper. An alarm rang from the direction of the courtyard, and I typed the rest of the letters as fast as I could find them.

The quick brown fox jumps over the lazy dog.

The sound of the last key hitting the roller echoed like surf slapping the shoreline. The sound faded away, but nothing happened. For a second my heart stopped hammering—had I done it wrong? Had I completely misunderstood Uncle Lem's message? Then came a tinkling, broken-glass sound, and the same fresh, after-the-rain smell from my father's vial, when I had opened it in the laboratory, seeped into the air. A hushed, gurgling sound grew. It was suddenly brighter inside the tree, and I leaned forward to look behind the typewriter: the tube had filled with blue liquid, the same color as the blue ink. In the new light, I could now see it went through the bark of the tree at just the right angle to connect to the water-light in the tunnel, twinkling like the surface of a pond on a sunny day. As it disappeared into the tunnel, the gurgle became a roar as loud as a waterfall. The tree shook, and I lost my balance and fell against the door of the fort. Jane opened it from outside, and I tumbled onto the ground.

The air was charged with energy—every blade of grass stood tall. The dirt at the base of the dogwood tree was glowing, and a blue strip appeared in a straight path that headed toward the museum, as if someone were painting a line from underground.

My foot sank into the soil, and a daffodil sprouted up. As the blue line charged toward the museum, flowers of all colors sprang to life in its wake.

I ran so fast my feet were wheels, Jane not far behind me. The blue line continued on a steady path, the underground roar almost deafening as the museum came into view. Flames licked out from the library window. The mayor was in the courtyard watching the smoke curl in the direction of the toolshed. Florence stood where Jane's cake had once sat. Uncle Renald stood nearby, his hands bound in magnetized gloves, his chin sunk onto his chest. They looked at me first, and then, with disbelief on their faces, their eyes tracked the path of spurting blossoms.

The mayor shouted, but I couldn't hear him over the noise. From the way his mouth contorted, it looked like, "Grab her!"— but none of his men moved. They stood agape as the blue line disappeared under the foundation of the museum. On the other side was the Mechanical Devices Room, dominated by the printing press. I tried not to imagine the press creaking and bending under the heat from the fire inside. The sounds of the fire and the roaring of the water were thunderous.

Then, silence.

A silence with a promise.

Then, an enormous explosion. Blue, sweet-smelling liquid gushed out of the museum like a fountain. There was suddenly no fire, no smoke, just calm, cooling water rushing and flowing into the courtyard and around the museum, soaking everyone to their knees.

The grass around the courtyard turned a brilliant shade of green, and flowers and berry bushes sprouted and grew at an impossible rate. Birds started singing—cardinals and bluebirds and waxwings—their normally subdued noises becoming a cacophony of joyful song. Mixed with the sound was the *beep beeping* of aer readers powering on.

The mayor's men waved their aer readers triumphantly above their heads. One of them removed Uncle Renald's gloves and then slapped him playfully on the back. Karl appeared from the direction of the toolshed, the mayor's man running after him, but when the water splashed onto their feet, they shouted like they'd found an oasis in the desert.

Jane had a beautiful smile on her face. She took the hedgehog out of her pocket and slipped him to Uncle Renald, who let out a whoop.

As the blue water drenched my shoes, I was filled with the strangest yet most comforting feeling that all would be well, the books would be saved, Uncle Lem would return, and I would somehow see my parents again. I was filled with hope.

CHAPTER

25

THE MUSEUM WAS A DISASTER. Two feet of water filled each room, but, strangely, as it receded, nothing was wet. Even the mangled, half-burned books in the library were as dry as when the mayor had first started the fire. The printing press—Old # One—had been spared.

The mayor and his men strolled around the courtyard as if they were tourists at the seaside, using their aer readers at full speed and, once in a while, pausing to take in deep gulps of air.

"It's so refreshing here," the mayor said, finally pocketing his aer reader. "So clean. It would have made an excellent site for the new family park. No, wait—" he went on, as Uncle Renald tried to say something. "I'm truly sorry for the misunderstanding earlier. In the future, let's address such issues before they get out of hand." It seemed that the water had made him as apologetic as he had earlier been intent on destroying the museum. Although he didn't exactly take the blame for the "misunderstanding."

Florence kept her eyes down as he spoke, raising them and offering a shy, rueful look.

"You lied to us," I whispered. "And stole from the museum." Jane came and stood by me.

"I didn't want to," she said. Her eyes flicked to the mayor. "I'm so sorry."

She had betrayed us to earn her father's approval. Under different circumstances we might have all been friends. I knew what it was like to make a bad decision about friendship, and to be forgiven.

A patch of newly blossomed flowers radiated color from the edge of the courtyard. I picked a sprig of hyacinth and twirled the stem between my fingers. "I never showed you the book of flowers in the museum's collection," I said. I could only hope it was still there, that her father hadn't destroyed it. I held the flower out to her. "Blue hyacinth, for sincerity. To remember to be truthful." It was the closest I could get to accepting her apology.

She took it from me with a small nod.

The mayor patted his pockets, watching the pools of water melting into the soil, the chipmunks frolicking in the leafy tree branches. His gaze landed on the hedgehog nestled in Uncle Renald's hood and his nose twitched. "Fascinating creature," he said, reaching out to pet it. "Maybe we should add a zoo to my initiative."

"I'm happy to show you out," I said, motioning down the path toward the front gate. "I'm sure you need to get back to town."

"Of course," he said. "Many thanks for your hospitality." Florence collected her suitcase from the dormitory, and the mayor and his entourage followed me to the gate, which was hanging in pieces from their arrival. "I'll send someone right away to repair this damage," the mayor said.

"Mr. Mayor," I said, "about the countdown for the museum reassignment—could you please make sure it's deactivated? Since everything is back to normal?"

"Normal?" he said. "Let's enjoy the fresh air for now. We'll worry about trivialities later." He cast an overlong glance in the direction of the museum, which was not at all reassuring.

The gate clanged as I closed what was left of it firmly behind them.

My aer reader worked lightning fast now. There were no messages from Uncle Lem, just an advertisement for a shop in town that had reopened. Nervous after the mayor's comment, I checked the status of the missing persons report—maybe the mayor hadn't tampered with it? Maybe it had been automatically reset by the Essence? But no, the countdown was still active, and worse, the mayor *had* changed it. There were two days left. Two days until I lost everything, unless I could find my parents.

Heading straight to the Mechanical Devices Room, I walked around the printing press slowly, even tried to crawl underneath, although I didn't fit anymore. I had forgotten about the spying game because more often my father and I used to pretend the press was a friendly dragon that had been asleep for a thousand years, guarding its treasure. The only way it would wake up and share its gold was if we made it laugh. We whispered it pun after pun, punctuated with giggles. I wish I could laugh now.

I looked up OLD # ONE on my aer reader and confirmed the story of the *Spy* printer. But there was nothing to tell me the significance of the clue. And what about the rest of the words? *Citrus* and *cerulean*—fruit and the blue of the sky? I checked the printing press for any mark that looked like a grapefruit, an orange, a lemon, or a lime. Nothing. In case *sky* meant "ceiling," I lay on the floor and looked up at the top of the Mechanical Devices Room. Nothing.

It was possible there was something in the code that I missed, something more on that page. Maybe the colon was important somehow. I needed to find my mother's book and figure it out.

The library was a huge mess again. Piles of books towered across the room, some simply splayed upside down, some half burned with crackly pages falling out of their spines. Thousands of books had been damaged or destroyed. Thousands I would never have a chance to read in the book handler. Countless bookmarks

I would never discover. My mother's book wasn't on the floor where I had last seen it, after Karl knocked it off the table. But it had to be here somewhere. I searched for it recklessly, accidentally knocking over a mound of books that skittered to the floor like a rockslide, until Jane put a calm hand on my shoulder and offered to help.

Outside in the courtyard, Uncle Renald sat at the stone table drinking cider and throwing a ball on a long string for his hedgehog to chase. Jane and I watched them through the library window as we gathered piles of book covers and loose pages, laying their dry, rumpled sheets on the center table. We sorted them into stacks of ones we had already searched, and used the book handler to return books that were undamaged to their shelves. I was very careful to use finger pads. The books felt a hundred times more fragile than before.

The hope that had sunk in through my toes had faded like the spreading ripples of a rock thrown into a pond. But the others seemed so happy. Jane hummed as she helped me. Karl walked by, and Uncle Renald stood up and offered his seat, pouring him a cup of cider. Then Uncle Renald took something out of his pocket and handed it to Karl with a short bow. Karl's aer reader. It hadn't been in his room for safekeeping after all. Uncle Renald scooped up his hedgehog, letting him scamper up and down his arm, and ambled into the library.

"What did you think about that water gush? It was even better than the fountain exploding!" Uncle Renald said. He smiled, showing a gap between his front teeth, one I had never noticed before because I had never seen him smile. He pushed aside a pile of books and sat on the table, swinging his legs. "Turned out to be a pretty nice day after all, didn't it?" he said, as Karl carried in the empty bottle and cups.

"Yes, sir!" Karl said, a grin breaking across his face as he headed toward the kitchen.

I couldn't say anything. It seemed like everyone was eating honeyed nougat and I had a bag of sand.

"Let me help you," Uncle Renald said, grabbing for the book closest to him.

"Don't!" I shouted, and he dropped the book back onto the pile, but it bounced off and smacked the side of a chair before landing under the table. "Please, don't help me," I said.

"Okay," he said, and wandered out of the room.

For hours, Jane and I continued searching and straightening. When she left and I was alone, I tried to keep going—we had made only a small dent. Most of the library still looked like a giant had picked the room up and shaken it. But soon exhaustion overcame me, and I slumped in a chair. My foot crunched something. It was the embosser the mayor had tossed aside—it had not fully escaped the flames. As I bent to pick it up, my insides felt how the metal now looked: melted and mangled, abandoned on the floor. I turned the embosser over and over, my distorted reflection spinning like a tin top, then shoved it in my pocket. My shoulders started shaking, and to stop them I put my head down on my arms on the table. But it didn't work. I cried so hard my face turned into a riverbed. I couldn't see, I couldn't hear, I couldn't smell. When I sensed a shift in the room, a changing from lightness to darkness, I drifted off to sleep.

I awakened with the top of my aching head warmed by a patch of morning sun, the sound of chirping birds and chittering squirrels in the courtyard almost deafening. Peeling my face off the table, I ran my pinky fingers across my forehead and down my eyes, trying to ease calmness into the throbbing. My vision was blurry when I opened my eyes, and, for a second, I saw my father in the library, carrying vials of brightly colored liquids, just as he had been doing the last time I saw him. Blue and orange liquids. Could that be cerulean and citrus?

When I blinked, the image of my father disappeared.

I took a deep breath and smelled honey and lemon, then heard a deep, familiar voice behind me.

"Good morning," Uncle Lem said.

I turned around so fast my head felt like a merry-go-round. Uncle Lem caught me and bundled me in a hug. "You're back!" I cried, and twisted to see behind him.

"I'm alone," he said.

Tears poured down my face again. I hadn't dared admit it to myself, but I had hoped against hope that Uncle Lem would some-how find my parents and bring them home. But he hadn't. Maybe he hadn't been looking for them at all.

Outside, Uncle Renald whistled cheerfully, scattering seeds for the birds.

I wiped my nose on my sleeve. "He hasn't been like this the whole time," I said, trying to gain control of myself. "Nothing like this."

"I know," Uncle Lem said. "It's the Essence. It resets people, brings all the good to the surface. It brings new life to everything. But you don't feel happy, do you?"

"I'm happy that you're back!" I said.

"But not happy like that?" He pointed out the window at Karl, who had climbed an apple tree and was bouncing its branches to loosen a fruit.

"No," I said. "I did at first. For a minute, maybe."

"It doesn't work on us all the same way," he said. "A tiny surge, at first. But it goes away almost instantly, partly because we've lived in such close proximity to the source." He looked around the room, shaking his head. "I'm sorry I wasn't here to help you. I tried to be back in time to replenish the Essence myself. I didn't expect it would run out so quickly."

"The Essence is the water," I said. I wanted him to know I knew.

"Yes." Uncle Lem tilted his head. "How much did Uncle Renald explain?"

"He didn't explain anything. Tell me," I pleaded. "Where have you been?"

Uncle Lem's eyes squinched together the way they did when we played chess and he was thinking about his next move, but with a sadness to them this time. "I was somewhere it's not always possible to go." He said it as quietly as a flower slowly drooping in the sun; there was something he was afraid to tell me. Something he probably should have told me long ago, when I first came to live at the museum and begged him over and over to help me find my parents.

He knew where my parents had gone. I waited for him to say more, needing him to say more and at the same time afraid of what he would say, but he turned away, reaching for a book with a curled cover and smoothing it gently.

"We have a problem," I said. "I made a mistake." I lowered my head and explained about the missing persons report.

Uncle Lem slipped his aer reader on immediately, seemingly for the first time in a while. It whirred with reports and messages, probably including the ones from me—he'd never gotten them until now. After examining the page for missing persons, he nodded. "It appears we do have a problem," he said. "One day? That's not much time. Not much time at all." He shook his head, opened his mouth, closed it, looked around at the disarray of the library, and finally said, "When was the last time you ate?"

If I was hungry, I couldn't tell—the ache in my stomach was a new kind of gnawing.

But as if on cue, Karl bounded into the room with bowls of steaming creamed wheat swirled with brown sugar, and Jane followed him with cups of orange juice and insisted we eat breakfast. Food was not normally allowed in the library, but nothing was normal anymore. As I took my first bite and Karl and Jane made their way outside to the courtyard, Uncle Lem straightened a nearby heap of books and then started talking.

"I owe you some information," he said, picking up his spoon. "Before we can figure out where to go from here. The Paper Museum is more than a museum. It was built to protect the Essence and the books. When society at large proved they couldn't handle magic and thus 'forgot' about it, some were allowed to remember, as the Essence was needed as an energy source—especially for the aer readers. A museum of paper artifacts became an ideal place for concealment, a place few people would visit, a place where a line of curators could care for the Essence."

The image of the ancient page from my mother's aer reader flashed in my mind. *To keep it safe for the world without the world knowing.*

"Nobody else knows about it?"

"Very few," he said. "The curators and their families—and, when necessary, a select group of close friends. Our job is to protect it but also to study it, to understand it. Essence particles float in the air and seep into the earth for years—decades, even centuries sometimes, although lately much shorter, before they finally ebb away. The supply must be replenished before the Essence runs out completely."

A spiral of steam lifted off Uncle Lem's spoon and dissipated into the library air.

"And I replenished it," I said, scared to think of what I had done. But of course that's what I had been doing in the dogwood fort. Uncle Lem had set up the typewriter with the tube connected to the Essence and had given me instructions, and I had done it. Only I had had no idea what I was doing. If I had known, I doubt my hands would have been steady enough to push the keys on the typewriter. Perhaps that's why Uncle Lem didn't tell me ahead of time.

"Why are we the curators?" I said, holding my spoon in midair. Uncle Lem kept eating. "Why our family?"

"Because certain ones of us are able to resist the effects of the Essence, and therefore manage it. Everyone else goes a little batty," he said, smiling. "Although that wears off, sometimes quickly, sometimes over a lifetime."

"Uncle Renald doesn't seem immune to it."

Uncle Lem wiped the side of his lip with his thumb. "His gifts lie elsewhere. He filled in for me because he's my sibling, but not everyone in our family is called to be a curator. No matter how much they want to be. And sometimes people from outside are called, such as your father. Curators are allowed to experiment with the Essence, to discover what else it can do. Some of us are more skilled at it than others."

"Is Uncle Renald allowed to experiment with it?"

"No," Uncle Lem said, dragging out the word. "He's not. Why do you ask?"

I told him about the "earthquake" and the blue smoke, about the hedgehog.

Uncle Lem stood and swung his arm to gesture that I should follow. He walked to Uncle Renald's room and pressed the button for the basement door. Our footsteps echoed down the stairs.

Nothing seemed damaged by the fire or the flood. Uncle Lem surveyed the room, glancing between the hedgehog's box and the giant basin now filled with round puffs of blue smoke swirling around like fireflies in a jar. "He shouldn't have done this," Uncle Lem said. "Especially when the Essence was ebbing low. That would explain why the Essence drained much faster than I calculated it would. If he hadn't used it, I would have been home before any of this could have happened."

"Why did you leave when you did?" I said, studying the blue fireflies to avoid meeting his eye.

Uncle Lem sighed. "I had to. Where I needed to go is only reachable when the Essence is stretched thin."

"You know where my parents went," I said, looking up.

Uncle Lem tapped at the edge of the basin, sending a blue firefly skittering away to the other edge. "I know where they were headed," he said bluntly, finally. "But not where they ended up. Your parents are a special type of curator called *gatherers*. They are in charge of gathering what is needed for replenishing the Essence. They go to—" he hesitated. "Special places and gather water. That water has magical qualities of its own, and what they collect is stored until the Essence is running low; then it is combined with the Essence under the museum. That is how the supply is replenished."

Water with magical qualities. The bottle of truth mixture I had found on my parents' bureau. The glass bottle that resembled the vials hanging above the well in the underground tunnel, each marked with a name and a number. Those were the special places they had taken water from. Names—of book authors. And page numbers.

"They go into the books," I said, testing out the idea the way I would prod an icy puddle with a stick to see if the thin frozen surface would break.

Uncle Lem's eyebrows darted up.

"I touched a book when I had Essence on my fingers," I said. "It showed me what was inside the book, for a second. I thought it was an illusion, but it wasn't, was it?"

"No," Uncle Lem said. "It was real. There is a world inside each book."

With those simple words, my own world shifted, expanded— just as a book cracked open unlocks into two connected sides. The prairie in the book, the canvas flapping soundlessly in the wind. That was *real*.

"What happened to the worlds in the books the mayor burned?" I asked, the memory of the smoke stinging my nostrils again.

"There are multiple copies of books," Uncle Lem said. "As long as one copy exists in our world, at this library or another, the book world is intact."

That is why Uncle Lem said the museum was to protect the Essence *and* the books. Without the books, those worlds could not exist, and the Essence could never be replenished.

"So my parents went into a book?" I said.

Uncle Lem nodded. "There is one rule about these trips that must not be broken. It was put into place centuries ago, when the museum was set up, along with a system of checks and balances, in case anyone at the museum ever tried to amass too much power. The rule is: nothing living can be brought back from a book. Doing so would trigger a notification to the office in power. The mayor's office."

"And my mother brought something back."

"Not intentionally. An insect of some sort landed on her shoulder, and she didn't notice until it was too late."

"They went back to return the insect?" I saw her hands shaking something into the tiny plasticress box.

"Yes, and I went to city hall to explain that it had been a misunderstanding. Although I'm not sure the mayor fully believed me. He has no idea about the Essence—he only knew an alarm had been triggered, which apparently put us on his watch list.

When I got back to the museum, your parents were gone, and I assumed they had returned from the book and gone home. That's when you showed up looking for them." He shook his head. "And when I put their tray away in the laboratory and found they hadn't retrieved their aer readers, I knew something unexpected had definitely happened. I was worried their attempting a second trip right away might be dangerous."

"What do you think happened to them?" I asked, my voice cracking.

"I'm afraid their path may have gone astray while passing from our world to the book world. There is a meeting point, in case anything ever goes wrong, and that's where I've been."

"What kind of meeting point?" I asked.

Weariness crossed Uncle Lem's face. "There is a waterfall where many rivers meet, far from here. It is a sister source of Essence, even more powerful than our own, but its location is so secret there are very few ways of getting there. Traveling through a book—which your parents are able to do—or by waiting until the Essence is thin enough to cross through. Unfortunately, I had to wait for the second option, which involved being away from the museum at a crucial time."

I imagined jumping across stepping-stones to a colossal waterfall, an arched gate nearby with green vines curling up its carved sides. The gate would open into a sun-drenched garden of vibrant colors, my parents waiting on the grass.

"But they weren't there," Uncle Lem said. "I'm so sorry, Lydia."

"How were they supposed to get there from the book? Maybe it's taking them longer than you thought."

Uncle Lem scratched his ear. "They carry a vial with them, a special tincture of waters taken from waterfalls, both from this world and from worlds in the books. To get to the meeting place, they would pour it into moving water. I don't know what delayed them from coming back, but we will have to be patient, again. And hopeful."

His words hit me like a slow-motion swarm of bees. "They don't have the vial," I whispered. "We found it under one of the bookshelves in the library."

"You did?" Uncle Lem asked, his eyes widening. I pointed with a heavy hand to the rolling cart by the cabinet, where the triangular bottle sat.

"Their embosser too." I pulled the twisted metal from my pocket and showed it to him.

"That does complicate things," he said, a hitch in his voice. "But your parents are resourceful. I'm sure they have a plan."

I focused on inhaling and exhaling as we went back upstairs into the long hallway, counting each thick breath, because where could my parents be? Were they trapped in some dark place with no way to get home?

Uncle Renald trotted by the window, holding his hedgehog, and Uncle Lem shook his head with a strained smile at the distraction. "It's nice to see the gentler side of him again," he said, and I knew he was trying to keep my mind off my parents. "He did love animals as a child. I must admit that I was not entirely at ease about leaving the museum in his care. He's always been a little miffed that he wasn't called to be Head Curator." I tried to focus on what he was saying, tried to push away images of my mother and father in a world with no door. "I cannot tell you how glad I am that he gave you the *Book of Essence* so you could replenish the supply. Did you have any trouble finding the page with the panel coordinates?"

I was so surprised I couldn't speak.

"He did give you the book, didn't he? Or did Karl give you the backup aer reader with the directives? I'm sorry I couldn't give it to you directly—it wasn't that I didn't trust you to hold it; I didn't trust the aer reader. It wasn't ready to be activated yet, but I knew it would be drawn to you."

I remembered the humming noise Karl's aer reader had made on the first day when he dropped it, before handing it over to his mother. "Neither of them gave me anything," I said. "I followed your instructions and typed what I always wanted to type."

Uncle Lem gave me a puzzled look, his mouth folded together.

"Remember, *The quick brown fox jumps over the lazy dog*?"

"I remember, of course," he said. "But where did you type it?"

"On the typewriter you left me in the dogwood fort."

He frowned. "I didn't leave you a typewriter."

"The green one," I said. "In the dogwood fort." I didn't know what else to say.

If he hadn't left it for me, who had?

There was only one answer: my parents. They had hidden it there for me to find before going on their trip—or before one of their previous trips, not knowing if and when I might need it—and they had left me the note. *Neither snow, nor rain, nor heat, nor gloom of night, stays these couriers from the swift completion of their appointed rounds.*

They were the couriers, on their rounds.

Delivering messages like the boxed text in the book with the pink ribbon. Old # One: citrus & cerulean. The drawing of the crowd gathered at the riverbank, the woman clenching her hand, the mix of people nearby. The birds and butterflies flying around, the polka-dotted bug on the table.

"Uncle Lem," I said slowly. "What type of insect landed on my mother?"

"I believe it was a ladybug," he said.

I knew where my parents were.

CHAPTER 26

"WE HAVE TO FIND that book," I blurted out, then raced to the library, Uncle Lem right behind me.

Frantically, I tore through the remaining piles of charred books and loose pages.

"It's the one with the pink ribbon!" I shouted.

"What a glorious day!" Karl said, waltzing into the room. But I felt fear, not happiness. If the mayor had burned that book, all was lost.

"Help me find it!" I begged.

Uncle Lem programmed a search on the book handler, and it began zipping across the bookcases, quickly but methodically checking every book left on the shelves. Karl danced between the tables, patting the tops of them and bending down to look under them.

Twenty minutes of searching felt like getting pierced a thousand times with thorns.

Karl pulled the trampled hedgehog cage from a corner. "Found this!" he said, holding it up. He swung it slightly before putting it back down.

"Wait!" I said. The book was seared to the underside of the cage. An ocean of relief surged through me. Karl peeled the book off, leaving a crisscross pattern on the front, and handed it to me. The entire first half of the book was now blank, whereas the first time I looked at it, only the beginning pages were blank. Pages were disappearing. Thankfully, the picture was as I remembered it, and as I looked at the woman petting the dog, the way that she held herself, even from the back, screamed that she was my mother. The slope of the man's shoulder next to her, partially on the page, was my father.

I held it out to Uncle Lem. "How do we get them out?" I asked. But they had given me the answer. "Old # One : citrus & cerulean." The printing press. The orange liquid from the birdbath and the blue Essence. We needed to do it fast, before any more pages—including the page they were on—disappeared.

It was a short distance from the library to the Mechanical Devices Room, but it had never seemed so far away. Uncle Lem and Karl were on my heels.

"Can I help?" Karl asked, as Jane came in with a bouquet of fresh flowers.

I looked over at Uncle Lem. Karl had probably already heard a lot more than he should have, if we meant to keep the Essence a secret, and now Jane would too.

But Uncle Lem nodded.

The printing press was directly over the well of Essence in the tunnel.

"What does it do?" Jane asked.

"It prints words and pictures on paper," I said. "Or it used to, anyway." A metal bar sticking out from the middle of the frame—a handle of some sort—was worn smooth, as if it had been pulled hundreds, maybe thousands, of times by printers' hands. The wooden frame itself was pitted with nail marks and covered in ink stains. I ran my hands around the outside of the printing press, examining all its pieces and markings.

"Are these letters?" Karl asked. Uncle Lem leaned in close to the flat section of the press where he was pointing. Several tiny metal pieces were grouped together, surrounded so tightly by squares and rectangles of wood and metal it took a minute to realize they weren't part of the original woodwork.

"I can't make them out," he said. "They've fused together."

A piece of sturdy canvas folded up from the flat part of the press, with adjustable pocket corners, forming a space for a piece of paper or a thin book. "We need a piece of paper," I said. "To test how it fits in."

Jane reached into her back pocket and pulled out her birthday message, the card Uncle Renald had confiscated. "He gave it back to me this morning," she said.

"Go ahead," Uncle Lem said.

I put the paper in, adjusted the pocket corners, and folded down the canvas. The blank side of the paper lined up on top of the tiny metal pieces. When I lifted the canvas back up, nothing had changed.

Jane kneeled next to the printing press, her pointer finger looping paths in the air as she studied the mechanics of the press. "We need to roll it through here," she said, indicating a crank under the square part of the press. "Then push on this." She stood and put her hand on the metal bar sticking out from the frame.

I wasn't sure how this would get my parents back. But as Jane pulled her hand away, a small ring stood out on the end of the handle—a book circle with the book faded into time? When I ran my finger over the design, it was too worn to tell for sure, but we needed to try.

"We need ink," I said. Karl pointed at one of the inkpots in the room, the contents of which had long ago dried up. I shook my head. Thinking of my parents trapped in that book for three whole months made the walls of the room tilt toward each other. To steady myself, I closed my eyes and imagined my parents in Uncle Lem's laboratory, mixing up a batch of blue and orange ink. "We need citrus and cerulean ink. And I know where to get it."

CHAPTER 27

THE GRASS ON THE path to the toolshed was thick and lush. A deer leapt around the border of the woods. When I reached the bird-bath, I took a glass jar I had grabbed from the kitchen and bent over to scoop up some of the orange liquid. But the birdbath was completely dry. The puddle of orange that had dripped down its side and pooled on the ground was gone.

I couldn't allow myself to panic. Racing to the dogwood fort, I barely had time to register that the tree and the ground seemed to be back to normal before I was in the fort and pressing the book circle to go down into the tunnel. The light from the Essence was now almost blinding. At the fork in the passageway, I paused to catch my breath. The two times I had opened the door under the birdbath, orange drops had fallen through. I could only pray there was some liquid left, and that I could catch it in the jar.

Positioning myself, I pushed the glass book circle embedded in the dirt. The door overhead slid open. And just when it seemed that nothing would come out, a single orange drop fell—*plink!*—into the jar.

As soon as the cover was screwed tightly on, I ran the rest of the way down the tunnel to the spot outside the underground laboratory.

The jars above the well were now empty, and the well was filled to the brim with Essence, the air resonant with melodic humming. I carefully unscrewed the lid of the jar and lowered it into the liquid like a spoon, then dripped a blue drop into the jar and quickly closed it again. I had put in one drop of each, but the entire bottom of the jar was now covered.

In the Mechanical Devices Room, the printing press seemed even bigger than before. I wasn't sure how to put the new mixture of ink into the press. Uncle Lem searched for a rag or something to dip into the ink and paint onto the metal pieces, but I couldn't wait that long. I tilted the jar and poured the liquid out. Some spilled on my fingers—the orange didn't sting or numb me this time. Combining it with the Essence gave it a new sort of power, and assuaged the burning sensation. The pieces on the printing press were metal, but the liquid soaked into them like a sponge.

I took Jane's card out of the canvas and slipped in the book with the pink ribbon, opened to the illustration, then adjusted the pocket corners.

I folded down the canvas to align the page, then turned the crank. With a creak of wood sliding on wood, the flat part of the printing press moved toward the part with the handle. When it was all the way in, I pulled the handle toward me with all my strength and pushed on the book circle.

Please work, I prayed. *You have to work!*

My heart was a book on fire.

Citrus and cerulean, and Old # One.

I unwound the crank until the flat section of the printing press was all the way out. When I lifted up the canvas, there was a familiar shape now imprinted on the page, next to the embossed circles: a matching circle. It wasn't raised, but it was the same exact symbol, in ink.

Uncle Lem pulled the book out, holding it by the corner. "Did we do it?" he asked.

The drawing had not changed, but a faint pulsing sensation emanated from the freshly printed circle on the page.

"What now?" Jane whispered.

Two matching circles. One a way in, one a way out.

I knew what I had to do.

"May I have the book, please, Uncle Lem?" I tried to keep my voice as calm as a pond on a windless day, because what I was about to do terrified me. But it was the only way left. Uncle Lem handed the book to me without question.

My hands glimmered where the blue and orange ink had dampened them. As I touched the newly printed circle, the air around me was again the first thing that changed, but instead of a silent, untouchable view like before, this time the scene swirled in a cyclone of noise and vibration.

It wasn't as cold as the last time, but the atmosphere was drizzled with wet from the river. I couldn't move. I was in the middle of the crowd of people, but none of them seemed to be able to see me or touch me. They pushed through me as they leaned toward the riverbank, cheering and whistling loudly in my ear. Uneasiness spread through my hands and out my fingertips.

"Mother! Father!" I shouted, swiveling around. Behind me, as if through wavy glass, I could see Uncle Lem's worried face. There was a weight on my feet; Karl and Jane were holding down my legs. I was between two worlds. One wrong move and I might be gone from both.

I wasn't sure if I was strong enough to do this. My arms felt hollow. A wave of pain rippled across my temple. But I couldn't give in, because it was up to me to do the rescuing. I couldn't see my parents, but they were here somewhere. I forced myself to look around: there was the table spread with food. My parents were to the side of it, according to the drawing. Although here, it wasn't exactly the same as the drawing. Everyone was moving around. Hats and dresses brushed through me.

The air was thinner here. It was getting hard to breathe.

"Mother!" I called out again, desperation seeping into my voice. "Father!"

I wasn't sure how long I could stay in the book.

My vision was starting to blur.

Faintly, in the distance, someone called my name. I strained to hear it again. "Lydia!" It came again, a little louder. Frantically I looked around, but I couldn't see either of them. Spots started appearing in front of me instead of people. The trees lining the river became one big splotch of green. I was fading from the book.

Two shapes loomed before me as I struggled to maintain my grip on this world. "Lydia!" It was them! I held out my hands, desperate that theirs would not only find mine but be able to touch me without going through me, as everything else in this world had. As I started slipping back into the museum, my hands jolted: my mother grabbed one hand, and my father the other, the blue-orange residue on my hands smudging onto theirs.

I couldn't tell if Karl and Jane were still holding my legs. I was twisting, getting sucked into a whirlpool of colored lights.

A massive heaviness weighed me down and spun me around. I clutched my parents' hands.

And then we were back in the museum, piled in a heap on the floor. Uncle Renald ran in, gleefully shouting, "Visitors!" I untangled myself and stood up, letting my vision come back into focus. Although in the illustration my mother had been wearing a dress that matched the style of those around her, she was now wearing the same clothes from the last time I'd seen her. Had my parents really been in the book the entire time? Had I been in the same room with them every day without knowing it? I rushed at them and hugged them. Behind me, I could hear the jubilant shouts of Uncle Lem, Jane, Karl, and Uncle Renald.

There was so much to say, I couldn't say anything at all.

When we finally stopped hugging, I thrust my parents' aer readers at them. "Turn them on!" I said. The sound of their aer readers reactivating was more beautiful than any song ever sung. My mother unclenched her other hand, which she'd held tight this whole time, revealing the plasticress box that once held the ladybug. She tilted something onto her hand, holding it out to me. Sitting on her curved palm like a baby robin in a nest was the L that was missing from my typewriter.

"Lydia," she said. "We never meant to leave you."

"Is it really you?" I asked. "You're back?"

"Yes," said my father. "We're home."

My mother hugged me again. "Thank you, Lydia. For finding us. For coming to get us. Only you could have done it."

"What happened?" I asked. "Why did you get stuck there?"

"A simple miscalculation," my father said, two red patches appearing on his cheeks. "On my part. I didn't mix enough Essence and Incandescence to reopen the door into the book wide enough. We didn't have much time to prepare, and I underestimated the amount the little critter—beetle—would require. We were stripped of some of our equipment as we went through."

Incandescence. Light and heat, where Essence was light and water. Did Incandescence come from the books, too—fire collected to counter the Essence? Opposites that worked together.

"Without the embosser and the liquids," my father went on, "we couldn't open a door to come back. Thank you for opening the emergency exit."

"It took me a while to find the right book," I said. "And to figure out your message. Couldn't you have made it a little clearer?"

My parents looked at each other. "It was dangerous enough making those black boxes," my mother said. "Anything more would have made the book deteriorate even more rapidly."

I gulped. They had been so close to disappearing for good.

"Books don't appreciate visitors with extended stays," my father added.

I held up the melted embosser. "We found it under a bookshelf."

"Oh dear," my mother said, reaching for it. "Looks like we'll need to make some adjustments."

"How do you use it?" I asked. "When you're in a book, how do you make a circle on a page? Doesn't the page disappear?" I hadn't seen pages or words in there.

"It hangs like a fabric curtain, so you pick up the edge. Didn't you see it?" my mother asked.

I shook my head. "Things were a little hazy."

"What you were able to do was extraordinary. It might be about time to start your gatherer training." My father put his arm around my shoulder and squeezed.

"A curtain?" Karl said. "Like a sheet? A sheet of paper? Is that why it's called that?"

My mother smiled. Then she and my father looked around at the parts of the room that had been touched by the mayor's fire. My father raised both eyebrows, but said nothing. Then he spotted the book with the pink ribbon, lying near the printing press. "Is that the book?" he asked. "I'd like to take a peek, if you don't mind. Been wondering who won that interminable boat race."

Jane picked up the book and turned to the page after the drawing, but didn't let him touch the book. "We don't want you popping back into it," I said, not kidding.

"We certainly won't," my mother said, taking my hand. "We intend to stay here with you for a very long time. Plus, it looks like the museum could use our help with a little fixing up." Uncle Lem nodded.

My father said, "But first let's get that ice cream."

"I love ice cream!" Uncle Renald shouted. "What a perfect way to celebrate!"

His hedgehog ran up to me and jumped on my foot. I picked him up and cradled him, looking around at the library and the books that had been saved, my parents finally home, my friends and Uncle Lem safe, my house and the museum ours again.

For the first time since Uncle Renald came to the museum, I couldn't have agreed with him more.

ACKNOWLEDGMENTS

As a longtime admirer of paper and books and libraries, it's pretty surreal to have a book of my own to contribute to a shelf. I am so very grateful to the many people who helped make this happen.

Thank you to critique group members for their insight and encouragement, including Lucia Zimmitti, Susan Carlton, Marianne Knowles, Joyce Audy Zarins, Brenda Bickham, and especially Elizabeth Gittens, who has been a steadfast friend not just in writing endeavors but also in life. I am indebted to Erin Latimer, who helped me transform this story, and to Wade Albert White, Kimberly Long, and Kendra Young, who generously offered feedback.

I owe enormous thanks to Tracy Marchini, my agent, who believed in this book and found the right home for it, and to Ardi Alspach, my editor, for loving Lydia and her story and making a real book for Lydia to live in.

Thank you to Hari & Deepti for their amazing and intricate cut-paper cover—I couldn't have imagined one more fitting. Thank you to the entire team at Union Square Kids and beyond, including Tracey Keevan, Melissa Farris, Whitney Manger, Julie Robine, Renee Yewdaev, Grace House, Kevin Iwano, Ellen Day

Hudson, Terence Campo, Dan Denning, Jenny Lu, Diana Drew, and Leo Costigan, for their copyediting, proofreading, managing, marketing, designing, and more.

Thank you to my parents for countless visits to libraries and museums, to Stephanie for her lifelong friendship and for always believing in me, and special thanks to Bill, Edie, and Stewart for their love and support, and for breakfast nook brainstorming sessions.

Thank you to Jim at the town transfer station for saving typewriters for me.

"Old Number One" is a real printing press. You can visit it at the American Antiquarian Society in Worcester, Massachusetts.

ABOUT THE AUTHOR

KATE S. SIMPSON is a librarian at a small public library. A fan of books, hot chocolate, and rainy days, she loves visiting museums of all kinds. She lives with her husband and two children in New England, along with two cats and five typewriters. *The Paper Museum* is her debut novel.